DEMON

(Kassidy Bell Series)
Book 3

Lynda O'Rourke

Copyright © 2016 Lynda O'Rourke
All rights reserved.
ISBN: 10: 1530245370
ISBN-13: 978-1530245376

First Edition Published by Ravenwoodgreys
Copyright 2015 by Lynda O'Rourke

This book is a work of fiction. The names, characters, places, and incidents are products of the writer's imagination or have been used fictitiously and are not to be construed as real. Any resemblance to persons, living or dead, actual events, locales or organisations is entirely coincidental.

This eBook is licensed for your personal enjoyment only. This eBook may not be re-sold or given away to other people. If you would like to share this book with another person, please purchase an additional copy for each recipient. If you're reading this book and did not purchase it, or it was not purchased for your use only, then please purchase your own copy. Thank you for respecting the hard work of this author.

Story Editor
Tim O'Rourke
Book cover designed by:
Tom O'Rourke
Copyedited by:
Carolyn M. Pinard
www.cjpinard.com

Also by Lynda O'Rourke

Drug (Kassidy Bell Series) Book 1

Dwell (Kassidy Bell Series) Book 2

This book is dedicated to Tim for always boosting me up when I thought I would never complete it.

Demon

Chapter One

I stumbled across the gravel driveway. Ben gripped my hand, his footsteps taking on an unnatural pace. I struggled to keep up. Glancing back over my shoulder, the Bishop's house began to fade beneath the thickening fog. I shuddered. A snapshot image of my friends and I clambering through the chimneys, trying to escape Alex, clouded my mind. It could have been the end of us – me, Jude, Raven, and Max. If Alex had got hold of us – then what? All this shit... this nightmare would be over with... finished. I wouldn't have to face what horror lay ahead for me... Demons. The VA20 – the Cleaners – losing myself to a Demon forever – none of that would matter now. Had I really just wished that Alex had killed me? Deep down, the answer was no. I still had that human instinct in me to survive – to keep going – to not give up. There had to be a way out of this. I just needed to find that way. I stared at Ben through the swirling fog. Only moments ago, he had killed Alex. Poor Alex. My heart wept for him. He had held his arms out to Ben and pleaded for help. He had become something abysmal – deranged – a creature from the depths of despair, dangerous yet innocent of what he had become. Alex had made the same choice that I had – a life-changing choice – a no-going back choice that had led him to his death – innocently volunteering his body for a drug trial. I didn't want to become that. I didn't want to suffer. To become someone to loathe – to pity – to be frightened of. How did it all go so horribly wrong? I had thought my life to be bleak. No money – no job – no prospects. But what did I have now – now that I had stepped through into Cruor Pharma believing that it would be better than a regular job? I hadn't gained anything – my life was worse. How dumb I had been. If only I had taken that cleaning job – if only I had seen through my despair and not given in to the easy option – the temptation of a get-out-quick card – easy money. I shook my head. I was angry at myself. But how was I to know that Cruor Pharma was run by Demons? That Doctor Middleton was injecting his volunteers with dark matter – some weird mix from six different Demons? How the hell would anyone know that? The crunch from the gravel under our feet stirred me from my thoughts. Where was Ben leading me? I needed my eyes to remain open when in his company. I had to keep reminding myself that this wasn't the real Ben who had helped me to escape the hospital. This was Ben's body with a Demon inside calling all the shots, and I had no idea if I could really trust him. I had to stay sharp and lock away all the horrendous deaths that seemed to follow me like a stalker. I had to harden my heart to stay strong – to stay alive.

The silence of the early hours and blinding fog was overpowering. I may as well have been wearing earmuffs and a blindfold. Ben was all I could see now as he dragged me through the still Ash trees out onto the empty lane by the red phone box. Where were the others? Where had Jude, Max, and Raven gone? I took some comfort in knowing that they had escaped the Bishop's house but how did I know that whatever the shadowy shape I had seen come into the hall and speak with Ben hadn't got them? What was it? Who was it? And how did it seem to know about me?

I pulled on Ben's arm, dragging my feet to make him stop. Taking a deep breath, I asked, "What was that shadowy thing in the hall you were talking to?"

Ben stopped abruptly, causing me to bump into him.

His jet-black eyes cut through the fog. "A Demon," he simply smiled.

"Does this Demon have a name?" I asked,

remembering the conversation my friends and I had had around the Bishop's dining table over dinner.

"It was Eras." Ben glared down at me.

I thought for a few moments. The names of the Demons the Bishop had mentioned went through my head like a shopping list until I came across the name Eras and mentally ticked it off. "So if that was Eras, who are you?"

"Quint," he grinned, reaching out and stroking the side of my face with his long, black, twisted nails.

I could feel myself tense as his sharp touch against my skin sent what felt like needles piercing through my flesh.

"Who is Doshia then?" I asked, trying to move away from his roaming nails.

The cloudy white fog almost seemed to turn into grey, swirling smoke as Ben or Quint loomed over me. His face seemed to stretch out of shape and take on a completely different appearance to that of Ben. I stumbled back and fell on my arse. My heart beat so hard I thought it was going to burst out of my mouth.

Quint stretched his arms down and his black nails dug into my flesh. "What do you know of Doshia?" He pulled me up so I was standing face to face with him. "Tell me."

"Not much," I glared back. "But I'm pretty sure it was Doshia who killed my friend, Hannah." I tried to pull away from Quint but his hands seemed to have an endless hold. His fingers had stretched and snaked their way around my arms like black vines. I felt my feet lift off the ground as Quint held me up like I was nothing more than a ragdoll. His dark, angry eyes bore into mine like he was searching for the truth inside my head – like he was seeing through my eyes and reading my inner thoughts.

Quint lowered his arms slightly, bringing me towards his face. "What did Doshia look like?" I could feel his hot breath against my lips. A searing pain shot through my head and behind my eyes. My vision blurred – or was it Quint's face that seemed to change? I couldn't be sure of anything other than the pain filling my head. "I want to know about Doshia – you tell me now!"

"I... I... you're hurting me... my head... what are you doing?" I felt my eyes shut. Or had I passed out? There was nothing but darkness – like I was lost inside myself. "Please stop... Quint... Ben... I can't stand the pain... it's blinding me..." My voice seemed a long way off as if it wasn't a part of me anymore. All of a sudden, Hannah jumping from her balcony filled my head. It was like I was there again – watching her fall – hearing her call my name and then the crunch of her body landing on her car. Then, as if on fast forward, I was hearing Doshia – *"Better run, Kassidy – I'm coming – Doshia is coming."* I could hear Jude's voice now – *"That's not Hannah – we have to go."* The pain inside my head had me spinning – I felt sick – I felt pissed. "Please just stop this… Quint… stop…" My voice was drowned out by Doshia. *"I know you… you thought I'd gone, but I've been with you all along."* Then, as if it had all been a dream, the pain left, my sight returned, and my feet were now standing back on the ground. I stared at Quint. He looked troubled. I lunged at him – my fists smacked into his chest.

I pushed and kicked and grabbed hold of his shirt. "Don't you ever do that to me again… I don't know what you were doing, but you fucking hurt me… that pain in my head… you did that… you made me watch my friend die all over again! You're a fucking arsehole." I turned away – blood pumping fast through my veins. I could feel myself shaking, my breathing laboured. "My veins," I gasped, yanking the sleeve of my top up. The thick, black fluid pulsed under my skin. It was like it had been activated. I could feel it moving. My heart thumped

— it hurt. I struggled to breathe. "What's happening?" I spun around and looked at Quint, only it wasn't him. Ben stood staring at me. His blue eyes misty through the fog. "Ben?"

He seemed to snap out of a trance, a frown on his face. Or was it confusion?

"Kassidy? Where are we...?" His voice trailed off into the fog.

"Ben, something's happening to me, my veins... I can't stop shaking... I can feel it moving through me... the VA20... it's moving." I looked down at my arm, the black fluid bubbled as it squeezed through.

"Sit down," ordered Ben, placing his hands on my shoulders. "You need to calm down, breathe slowly... in, out... in, out." He crouched down beside me.

I trembled, fearful that any sudden movement may send it racing faster. "What's it doing to me?"

"I don't really know," he said, taking hold of my arm and gently rubbing his fingers over my veins. "But it's slowing. It seems to reduce its flow when your pulse slows. Just sit quiet for a few minutes." He stood up and looked around him. "The fog is getting worse. We need to move on soon. Do you feel better?"

I stared up at him as he brushed down his waistcoat and straightened up his shirt. "A bit shaky still." Peering through the fog, I could just make out the red phone box but nothing more. That familiar feeling of something bad crept through me. I had felt it when I'd walked through the canteen at Cruor Pharma. I knew what drew close. I looked up at Ben.

"The Cleaners are coming," we both said to each other as if our thoughts were entwined as one.

Ben pulled me up, holding me steady, I wobbled on my feet. My heart rate had slowed a little, but that inner sense of dread kept it just above its normal beat.

"We need to get out of this fog," whispered Ben. He spun around as if searching for the right way.

I grabbed his arm as he took a step back towards the Bishop's house. "Not that direction. We've just come from there. I think we should go this way." I pointed through the fog, not really knowing if it would take us out of this village, or if it were even safe, but it had to be better than heading back to the house where all those dead police officers lay.

Ben turned and stared at me. "Can you

run?" He took hold of my hand. "Kassidy, we need to outrun the Cleaners. They've caught up with you, just like I said they would. We need to put as much distance between us and them."

I nodded my head. "Yes, let's go." My eyes darted left then right. I peered over Ben's shoulder into the fog, fearful that I would see those black shadows of the Cleaners emerge from the murky haze. I felt so vulnerable from all directions – not being able to see what lurked in this miasma. I reached down under the neck of my top and pulled out Father Williams' cross. It glinted in the gloom. It wasn't much protection, but it may be enough to stop the Cleaners and give me some time to get away. Yanking on the strap of the satchel to make sure it was secure over my shoulder, I let Ben take the lead. We ran blind.

CHAPTER TWO

We hadn't been running long when Ben stopped dead in his tracks. The fog still swirled around us like an angry swarming crowd, trying to keep us contained within its cold, icy grip. The sound of muffled whispers filtered through on the air. I huddled close to Ben, my fingers clinging tight to his shirt – my face almost buried against his chest. I didn't want to see what, or who those haunting voices belonged to. I wanted to shut my eyes and hope that whatever it was would just go away.

"What is it?" I whispered, afraid of Ben's answer.

"Shhh," Ben said, wrapping his arms about me like a protective shield.

The whispers came again, only this time closer. The sound of footsteps along the lane seemed to stop, start, then stop again like they were lost in the fog. I pulled away from Ben. "That's not the Cleaners," I whispered. "They don't have footsteps, they glide."

"Wait." Ben snatched my wrist. "We don't know who it is – it could be the police."

"They're dead – Alex killed them all back at

the Bishop's – with your help," I whispered.

"What?" Ben frowned at me.

"You opened the door knowing that Alex would kill them all. I don't know how you did it, seeing as you were pinned to the ceiling with me, but you somehow opened the door," I said, trying to pull away from his hold.

Ben stared down at the ground and nodded his head slowly as if this was all news to him. He took a deep breath and whispered, "I don't remember."

"Well you did," I said. "So whatever is whispering and making footsteps can't be the police."

"There's always more from where they come from, Kassidy." Ben glared, pulling me back towards him. "Inspector Cropper has plenty of bodies to work for him."

I looked up into his blue eyes. "Do you really not remember what happened at the Bishop's? You really don't have any knowledge of that bloodbath – that massacre? Because that's what it was."

Ben stood silent for a few moments. He looked puzzled – his memory obviously blank. "Whatever I did, I must have done it for you – so don't stand there with that accusing look over your face. Did I save you from being a part of the body count?"

"Yes... but..." I stammered, trying to find the right words. "That doesn't excuse the fact that I'm only caught up in this shit because you injected me with VA20."

"So you don't want my help then? You don't want me to stay?" Ben let go of my arm.

"No," I spat, suddenly feeling angry at Ben's attitude and lack of guilt. "I don't need you."

Ben shrugged and turned slowly away, his head bent down.

Cursing myself for being emotionally weak, I reached out and took his hand. "I don't want you to go – I do want your help."

Ben shook his head and groaned. "Kassidy... you know you've just told the Demon in me that you want him... you want him to stay..." Ben cupped his hand under my chin, and a tiny ripple of black swam across his eyes. "You need to remember it's not just me you're talking to... you're dealing with a Demon... I'm not always Ben."

I reached up and took hold of his hand. "I don't care anymore. I'll deal with the Demon when he shows up and I'll deal with you when you're with me." I pulled away from Ben and let my hand slip from his. Was I making a big mistake having

Ben and Quint stay with me? That little voice of reason inside my head told me it was better to have them close and know what they were up to than have them working alongside Doctor Middleton and the Cleaners. Having Ben with me might just get me into Cruor Pharma's sister company and a chance to speak with Doctor Langstone. And if it did all fuck up, then hopefully Ben or Quint would help me. It was all *ifs* and *maybes*, but right now I didn't see much hope of doing it all by myself. And besides all of that, those feelings I had been having about Ben were niggling away at me. Every time I looked at him, I wanted to kiss him – feel his lips on mine. It was like a temptation I had never felt before – a dangerous one. But I just couldn't seem to shake it off.

The footsteps had come closer and my attention swapped from Ben to the approaching sound of clattering feet. I strained to hear what the whispering voices were saying.

"It's not my fault I can't run as fast as you two wearing these shitty shoes with bows on them."

I smiled to myself. For once I was glad to hear Raven's voice. She appeared through the fog, followed by Jude and Max. They stopped abruptly when they saw me.

Max gasped. "Shit, you scared me." His look of fright was replaced with a big smile. He held open his arms and hugged me. "I thought we'd lost you for good."

"I thought you'd fucked off and left us to face Alex by ourselves," hissed Raven, her face nothing more than a scowl. "Where did you go?"

"Ben saved me from Alex and the police," I said, suddenly aware that maybe this news wouldn't go down well with my friends.

"That's big of him," mocked Jude. He looked over my shoulder as Ben stepped forward from out of the fog. "You've saved her – now you can fuck off back to Cruor Pharma and start the next wave of injections. I'm sure Middleton has already got volunteers lined up for the next drug test."

"Hey... it's okay," I said, holding up my hands as if to offer a sign of peace. "I know you don't trust Ben, and I don't blame you, but..."

"Trust him? It's more than just trust..." spat Raven. "He's a psycho killing Demon. We turn our backs on him for just a second and he'll be having a fucking party inside our bodies." She stamped her foot down like a child having a tantrum.

"You might have charmed Kassidy with your snaky ways but it doesn't work on the rest of us," snapped Jude, "We. Don't. Want. You." Jude stood face to face with Ben, his face wrought with anger.

"Now just hold on, Jude!" I shouted. "I do have a voice of my own and I can make decisions for myself. I haven't been charmed or manipulated by Ben or anyone – I'm not a fucking child… he helped…"

"He helped because he wants you all to himself," cried Jude, spinning around to face me. "Can't you see what he's up to?"

"He's got to you so he can get to us," hissed Raven, jumping into the argument. "And when he's worked his charms on us then he gets the Cleaners and they get our bodies – before you know it – we'll all be devil slaves."

"Piss off – now!" shouted Jude, facing Ben again.

I looked at Max who stood just behind me. If I was going to stand any chance of convincing Jude and Raven, I would need to persuade Max. Grabbing hold of him by both arms, I said, "Please, Max, you know I wouldn't do anything stupid – you know I have my head screwed on, right? Ben can help us – I know he can. We need him. He can get us into Cruor Pharma where Doctor Langstone works. He might know more about your brother. We stand more of a chance of getting help from Doctor Langstone if we have Ben with us… please."

"I don't trust Ben, and neither should you," said Max. "But I do trust you."

"Then tell Jude and Raven – they won't listen to me." I let go of his arms and pushed him forward. "Tell them."

"Jude," said Max, "calm down and listen to me. All this shouting and arguing isn't going to help. We need Ben to get us into Doctor Langstone's place... we need..."

"We don't need shit from him," spat Raven, her voice full of venom.

Ben, who had stood quiet, pushed through Jude and Raven. He stopped beside me and turned to face the others. An icy chill breeze swarmed around us.

"You don't stand a hope in hell if you think you can just stroll in and see Doctor Langstone without me," said Ben. "I'm coming with you, whether you like it or not. While you stand here arguing, the Cleaners are gaining on you. Can't you feel them – feel their presence? They won't give up – their relentless hunting will never stop until they have you."

"We can get away from the Cleaners without you!" shouted Jude.

"But you can't get away from me," smiled Ben. "Kassidy told me she wants me to stay."

Ben turned and grinned at me. It was then I realised that Quint had come back – gone were Ben's blue eyes. Now all that stared back at me were two black eyeballs. His body almost seemed to be surrounded with a dark aura and his fingers had taken on that stretched, twisted, vine-like appearance. He snapped his arm forward and took hold of Jude, pushing him down to the ground so he was in a kneeling position.

"Stop it!" I yelled. "Don't you hurt him."

Quint took no notice of me. It was like I didn't exist. I watched as Jude struggled to get up.

"You don't want me to go with you. Well what are you going to do about it?" Quint stated more than a question. "Are you going to fight me?"

Jude stared up at Quint, his face dark with anger. "I'd love nothing more than to end you..."

"I feel a *but* coming..." smiled Quint. "Is there something stopping you?"

"Hey, Jude," Max suddenly piped in. "Best not argue with *it*. We've all seen what these *things* can do."

Quint snapped his head round and stared at Max. "*It – things?* I'm more than that – more than you'll ever be." He stretched his other arm out and snatched Max around the throat.

"Stop this – stop it – they're my friends and

if you hurt them, I'll kill you myself!" I screamed, punching Quint in the chest. "Let them go – now!"

Quint released them both. He stepped back, a smile stretched across his face. "Are we ready to go? Or do you want to wait for the Cleaners?"

I stood shaking. That awful feeling of VA20 pushing its way through my veins had started again. I pulled the sleeves of my top up and watched as the thick, black fluid simmered and popped like a muddy bog. I tried to calm my breathing.

Snatching me by my wrists, Quint smiled. He looked down the length of my arms and his black eyes shimmered.

Pulling away from him, I turned and faced my friends. "Look, I don't like this any more than you do... but... I think we need him. I want to see Doctor Langstone and get this shit out of me... it's getting worse and I think we stand a better chance if we have Ben or Quint... with us."

"If we ever make it that far," spat Raven, "which is highly unlikely with some Demon guy tagging along."

"Tagging?" glared Quint, bending down so his face was in front of Raven's. "I'm leading, not tagging."

I looked at Jude. He stared over his shoulder

into the thick fog, then, turning round and brushing off the dirt on his trousers, he said, "Let's just get going, we're not safe here." He pushed past me and disappeared into the fog.

Raven went next, followed by Max, who rubbed at his neck where Quint had grabbed him.

"Don't you ever attack my friends again." I glared, staring through the fog, not wanting to look at Quint. "Or I'll change my mind."

"You can't change your mind," said Quint, walking behind me. "You don't want to change your mind – you like me – I sense it."

"I like Ben – not you!" I snapped. I continued to move forward, slightly uncomfortable at having Quint behind me where I couldn't see what he was up to. He had gone quiet. I wasn't sure if I liked that or if I would rather have him sounding off. The uneasy feeling I felt was too much to bear and I spun around to see what he was doing.

"Keep up with the others, we don't want to lose them in this fog."

I was relieved to see two blue eyes staring back at me intently. Quint had disappeared for now, and for that I was grateful. If Ben could stay as Ben then maybe Jude, Raven, and Max could accept him – could see that it wasn't really his fault and that he was trying to help us. I knew I was walking a thin line having Ben travel along, but if Doctor Langstone could somehow remove VA20 from us then maybe he might help Ben. But that feeling of dread had me second-guessing myself again. This could all go horribly wrong if Quint took over Ben once and for all – then what? What was Quint's real intention? Was his plan to get us all together so he could have control over the Cleaners and use our bodies? But he could have done that already – we were all together now. Maybe he was waiting for us to find Robert – Max's brother. Perhaps just the four of us wasn't enough to gain control of the Cleaners. How many bodies were needed? My head swam with questions – it felt as thick as the fog I walked through. I felt Ben's hand slip over mine. I looked up at him as he walked beside me.

"We need to speed up," he said. "Let's get out of this fog."

I held his hand tight as we started to run. The cold air stung my eyes and nipped at my face. I felt safe when it was just Ben. He seemed strong and had a firmness about him like someone in authority. Perhaps that was the doctor in him? But what did that matter when there was a Demon lurking inside? Being strong hadn't been enough to fight off Quint. Was there anything or anyone who could wrestle off a Demon and come out smiling? I didn't think so. But I wanted to believe that something could be done – that there was a way of reversing the damage. Was I being naïve – losing my way? Only time would tell, and as we caught up with the others I knew I had to hang on and keep going. We all had to. Because if one of us fell, then we all would fall.

CHAPTER THREE

The fog had become patchy. Small snippets of the country lane we ran along revealed itself, then disappeared in a sudden blur, covered by a misty veil. To me, it meant that we were outrunning the Cleaners, escaping their foggy reach. Another break in the blindness presented the lane spilt into four directions. A crossroad. Max pointed up at a white, flaky road sign.

"That way will take us back in the direction we first started out from." Max looked to the right. "That leaves us with going left towards some place called Broken Head, or we could keep going straight and go to the town of Rane."

"Rane." Both Ben and Jude answered together. Then stepping across the road, they both took the lead.

I looked at Max. He shrugged his shoulders at me like he didn't have a clue and trudged forward. He looked tired. Dark shadows circled his eyes and his long hair stuck to the side of his face, damp from the cold fog.

Raven stepped in front of me. "Are you just gonna stand there, or what?" She bent over slightly so she could peer into my face. "There isn't time to stand about daydreaming you know, not unless you wanna become one of the devil's hands."

"Get outta my face, Raven," I mumbled, not in the mood for her dark ramblings. I stepped to the side and pushed past her.

"I don't know why you've let that killer join us, but I hope it's for a good reason and not because you've been tempted by him," she glared. "We've got this far without him, he's not needed for anything."

"He is needed," I snapped, continuing to walk across the road onto the lane ahead. "He'll get us in to see Doctor Langstone. I thought that's what you wanted? A chance to get rid of this drug!"

Raven grabbed hold of my arm and pulled on it. "But you can't trust a Demon! In fact, how do we trust anyone?"

"What do you mean?" I stopped dead in my tracks. "Are you talking about the others, Max and Jude?"

"Yes," she glared.

"Why?"

"We don't know either of them, do we?" she hushed, looking in their direction. "How do we know that Max's story about his brother is true?"

"Because he has his brother's passport

that's why," I said.

"Is it though? He could have just pulled out that passport on Ward 1 and claimed it to be his brother's and then fed us with some lie about his surname being different because they don't share the same father."

"That's just rubbish, Raven." I shook my head. "Max is a good guy, why would he suggest going to the Bishop's in search of his brother if he isn't really his brother?"

"Because he's a Demon," she hissed. "He read in Father Williams' diary that Robert, Alex, and Sylvia had headed to the Bishop's."

"So?"

"He obviously thought that all three of them were like us, able to house those filthy Cleaners, and knew the more bodies he had, the more chance there was of him claiming them."

I stood silent for a moment. This was too much. Max was nice. He was kind. I hadn't seen anything strange about him or had any doubts about him since we had first met. Raven was just talking out of her arse again. She didn't trust anybody. My thoughts were interrupted by a memory of Ward 2 where Max had first told us that he had volunteered because he needed the money to save up for his own place. That had been a lie.

Did Raven have a point?

"Well, what about Jude?" I asked. "I know you don't like him but that isn't enough to point the finger of blame in his direction."

"I just don't trust him," she whispered. "And he doesn't have any black veins. He doesn't seem to have had any reaction to VA20."

I chewed on my lower lip. I contemplated what Raven had just said. "Ahh, but Max does, so that rules him out," I smiled, relieved to have Max in the clear. But what about Jude?

Raven looked over her shoulder and pushed me in the back. "Come on, we need to keep moving. I don't know about you but I'm sure the devil's hands are on the move." She nodded in the direction we had just come from. The fog seemed to be rolling slowly forward.

I carried on walking, Raven followed beside me. She did have a point about Jude and his lack of reaction to VA20. But when I thought about what had happened on Ward 2, I remembered that May didn't have any black veins either. Poor May. I shuddered as my mind recalled how Wendy had ripped open May's throat and killed her. Pushing those thoughts away, I said, "Jude wasn't the only one who showed no reaction to the drug. May didn't either."

"What about that porter, Fred Butler? Funny how he died shortly after we left him – or should I say after Jude left him," hissed Raven. She continued to look over her shoulder at the fog. "We left him very much alive but was he alive after Jude had gone back into the locker room?"

"There was no reason for Jude to kill Fred Butler," I said, picking up pace. I didn't want to fall too far behind the others who were now quite a ways ahead. "We had him tied securely and gagged. Besides, you saw Jude when all that shit happened on Ward 2. He was fighting all the other volunteers – the ones who had turned crazy. He helped to get us all out of there. So if he was one of the Demons, why would he have bothered?"

"Because he wants us all to himself – he wants to be top Demon – we wouldn't be any good to him if we got killed by those other freaks on Ward 2. That's why he helped us to escape – I can sense it!" Raven shuddered and wrapped her arms about her. "And don't forget it was Jude who didn't want to go to your friend's house or the Bishop's at first. He kept trying to persuade us to go to his place in Wales. And, let's not forget he wasn't too keen on visiting Doctor Langstone. Jude was worried that we would get taken over by Langstone. See! He doesn't want anyone else to have us — he wants the power!"

"That still doesn't mean he's one of the Demons," I said, looking back over my shoulder. The fog seemed to have slowed, it lingered back across the lane. I let out a big sigh. I could feel my heart steady with the satisfaction that we were creating some distance between us and the Cleaners. Raven's suspicions about Jude and Max, though, left an uneasy feeling deep inside me. It was like a seed had been planted, and the more I thought about what she said, the more its roots pushed further down. I clutched onto the satchel, remembering the iPod inside. I'd had my doubts about all of them back at Hannah's flat. Someone had turned off the power preventing me from seeing what was on that iPod. But which one of them had turned off the switch? Maybe it had been done by accident? That's what I preferred to believe. But was I just trying to sedate those fears that one of us wasn't just a plain old human — one of us was made of something else, something dark and malignant? I shook my head. I was letting my brain get carried away from listening to Raven and her usual dark thoughts. Besides, Jude and Max hadn't shown any Demon qualities; far from it. Jude had revealed a completely different side to him the other night. I could feel my cheeks flush as

I remembered what I nearly let happen between us. No, I didn't want to believe that Jude and Max were bad. We had volunteered together, escaped together, and helped each other, and now here we were, trying to find an end to all this shit together. I nodded my head as if trying to convince myself that I was right to believe that. Yet still, that niggly little doubt stayed nestled deep inside. I looked ahead and could see the others had stopped at a bend in the lane. As Raven and I got closer, I looked at all three of them and my eyes fell upon Ben. If there were anyone amongst us who couldn't be trusted, I would have to point my finger at Ben. After all, I knew what lived inside of him – Quint.

CHAPTER FOUR

Mellow rays of sunlight poked through the clouds, allowing us a little warmth. Running through all that fog had left me feeling damp and a little cold. We stood just on the outskirts of Rane, taking shelter from any prying eyes that might happen to come by, behind a large, bramble hedge which skimmed the edge of the lane.

"Are we all sure we want to find Doctor Langstone?" asked Jude, straightening his shirt and running his fingers through his hair. "We all know it's a risk — a big risk to take."

Raven suddenly nudged me in the arm, her eyes darting over to Jude as if to remind me of her suspicions about him.

"It's a stupid risk," said Ben, stepping forward. "He is a Demon and just because he left Doctor Middleton to his drug tests, doesn't mean that he's safe."

"It was you who put that idea into my head, Ben," I said. "Remember, before you left me outside the canteen back at Cruor Pharma?"

"That was just me trying to make myself feel better for what I'd done to you. I have no doubt in my head that you will never get any help from Doctor Langstone. He can't be trusted," snapped Ben.

"Can't be trusted like you, you mean?" sneered Raven, peering out from under her straggly hair.

"But you haven't seen Langstone since he left, which I'm guessing was ages ago," said Max. "He could be different now. The fact that he left Middleton to pursue his messed up drug trials surely shows a lack of interest in gaining Demon power or whatever it is that you Demons are after. You can't be sure."

Ben shook his head. "I forget a lot. I only remember what the Demon in me wants me to remember. Sometimes, when I'm stronger, the past becomes clearer. I admit, I'm messed up. I'm a danger. And because I know I'm a danger, I know that makes Langstone a danger. You have no idea what goes on inside my head. Even though my Demon is quiet at the moment – it doesn't stop me from wanting to hurt you all. There's a lust inside me to kill, an urge to corrupt you – anyone who crosses my path – anyone out there will do. But you especially." Ben stared into my eyes. "The things I could do to you. I want to play you – I want to take you – I want to..." He took a step towards me. "But the real me – plain old Doctor Fletcher –

he's still here. I'm fighting those urges." He spun around to face Max. "I know Langstone feels like me. Anyone with a Demon inside them will. So I'm sure Langstone will take one look at you lot and all those Demon instincts will overwhelm him. You don't stand a chance."

Jude looked at me. "Why the fuck did you let him come with us? You've heard it from his own mouth. This guy is a danger, and while he's travelling the country with us, we're all in the shit."

Ignoring Jude, I said, "Right now, we're carrying a death sentence around with us. I'm going to go and see Langstone, with or without your help." I stared back at Ben with the same cold stare he was giving me. "I have nothing to lose. This kind of life – living on the run isn't for me. For all I know this shit in my veins could kill me off today, tomorrow, or next month. I don't know. But, from how I see it, Langstone is the only choice – the only chance of living again. So if he kills me off – then so be it." I pushed past Jude and stomped past Ben without as much as a glance. Stepping out onto the lane, I followed it to the left, toward the town of Rane.

"Wait up, Kassidy," called Max, running up behind me. "I'm coming, too. It's a chance *I'm* willing to take. I want to find Robert." He held up his arm. "This stuff inside me is moving. I keep feeling it. It's like an underwater current that makes my heart race – it's horrible."

"I know," I whispered, gently running the palm of my hand down his arm. "I feel like the clock is ticking for us – like it's only a matter of time until... until it's too late. We *have* to see Doctor Langstone."

"Hey, if we're really going to do this suicide mission then we need to plan this right," Jude suddenly piped in behind us.

I turned around, surprised that he was coming. "I thought you were dead-set against the idea. What's changed your mind?"

"I can't let you go it alone. We're in this together and I did make you a promise the other night, didn't I?" His eyes twinkled at me.

Feeling embarrassed at the mention of the other night, I looked down at the ground. But it was true. He had promised me that he wouldn't let anyone take me – he would look after me – all of us.

"And I can't leave you with that arsehole," Jude muttered, rolling his eyes back as if to point out Ben who walked slowly behind. "I won't let him take you."

My heart skipped a beat when I realised

that Ben was obviously going to come with us. But still unsure of his true intentions, it left me with that nagging feeling of who could be trusted. I looked over at Raven who trailed just behind Jude. She nodded at me with that knowing look as if to say – *see* – none of them could really be trusted. That they all had the potential of being a Demon and had a vested interest to keep us together. But what choice did I have except to trust their stories? For now, I didn't want to believe such things. Becoming suspicious of everyone in our group would only lead to more problems. Maybe even push me into making wrong decisions which could prove fatal.

CHAPTER FIVE

We stood inside a small ticket office at Rane Railway Station, which was on the outskirts of town. It had been our first opportunity of travel – escape. We hadn't had to go sneaking through the roads of Rane and avoiding the people who lived and worked there. It had been the ideal situation. Anyone who came across us would no doubt have seen that there was something not quite right about us. The only two travelling amongst our group who looked normal were Jude and Ben – well, Ben as long as he stayed as Ben and didn't suddenly flip over into Quint. I could quite easily keep my black veins and twisted nails hidden by pulling the sleeves of my top down over my hands. Raven was still covered up with Hannah's leather jacket – ever fearful that someone would see her flowery top. Mind you – looking at her shadowy face and long greasy hair, might scare someone. But poor Max only had his jeans and a ripped *Hellraiser* T-shirt on. There was no escaping the sight of his thick, black veins, and even if his veins did go un-noticed, there was no getting away from the fact that we all wore a haunted, shocked look about us. Traumatised – disturbed, was probably a better description.

Looking up at the timetable pinned to the wall, I could see that the first train wasn't due for another twenty minutes. The clock outside the ticket office had chimed 7 o'clock. I wondered how many passengers would soon be walking through the doors, ready to start their day of work. How many of them would notice us.

I turned away from the timetable. I felt on edge. This twenty minutes felt more like hours.

"Should we wait on the platform?" I said, heading for the door.

"I don't think that's a good idea," grumbled Raven. "You know what happened to that priest after he left the Bishop's house." She held up her hands and did an impression of the priest throwing himself in front of the train.

"That's not even funny, Raven," I snapped. "Don't tell me that shit. I'm already on edge as it is."

"She does have a point, though," said Jude, coming away from the front entrance. He had been keeping watch – checking for any signs of the Cleaners or the police. "As much as it pains me to say it, Raven's right. We need to be very careful." He spun around as if looking for something. "Don't they have any of those vending machines here? I'm bloody starving."

"Is that all you can think about – food?" I moaned. "Is that your idea of being careful?"

"There's one just outside the men's toilet," said Max, looking at his reflection in the ticket booth window. He ran his fingers through his hair and tried to smooth out the strands. "But it only takes coins and we don't have any."

"I'll go check it out," grinned Jude, disappearing around a corner.

"Hey, do you think he's all right?" whispered Max, casually looking over at Ben, who sat on a wooden bench. Then back at me, he added, "He doesn't say much, does he?"

I shrugged my shoulders and was about to reply to Max when Raven cut in. "Of course he's not all right, he's the reason we're all here. He's a dirty Demon with evil thoughts going through his head. He's probably sitting there looking quite innocent but really he's planning which one of us he's going to *fuck* over first!"

Ignoring Raven, I spied a quick glimpse at Ben. He had done nothing but sit there and say nothing ever since we had arrived at the station. He just sat and watched. Watched us. Listened to us. I wondered what was going on inside that messed up head of his. Was he struggling to keep

Quint away? Was his silence his way of keeping Quint under control? Or was Quint hiding just under the surface like a wild animal stalking its prey – waiting? His moody stare was unnerving – intimidating almost. But maybe that was just armour – a shield – a *don't mess with me because deep down I'm struggling here* look. If I pushed away the horrible things that Ben had been a part of, I realised that his life couldn't be so great. He shouldn't even exist. How must it feel to be here with us, a group of people he didn't even know? A group who had already started to bond in some ways. I guessed Ben felt like an outsider.

Don't feel sorry for him, that little voice inside my head said. But I did.

I was about to go and sit down beside him when he suddenly stood up and walked over to the front entrance and looked outside. He was checking the time.

"We should wait on the platform," he said, turning to face me. "The train will be here soon – we don't want to miss it." He rolled back his shoulders and straightened up his jacket. He looked like someone on their way out for dinner with his smart waistcoat and suit – completely different to the scrubs he'd worn at Cruor Pharma. His eyes caught my stare – looking him up and down. He returned the same gaze. I turned away.

Jude sauntered back into the ticket office, his arms full with crisps and chocolate bars. "Grub up, everyone."

"How did you get them?" asked Max, swiping a bag of crisps from the pile in Jude's arms. "You didn't use the notes we had, did you?"

"Of course not," grinned Jude. "What does it matter anyhow? We've got to eat. I just broke the lock off the back of the machine and helped myself. Food and booze should be free – why pay?"

"You're a fool," snapped Ben. "Don't you see you're leaving a trail behind you? Someone's going to see that the machine has been broken into and then they'll check the CCTV and see us waiting in here for the first train. You've just given away our mode of transport and the direction we're travelling in."

"It's just some fucking food!" snapped Jude. "At least I'm looking after everyone – feeding them. What the *fuck* have you done to help?"

The lights in the ticket office started to flicker and hum. We all looked up at the same time. Ben walked back over to the front door and peered out.

"The fog is coming." He looked back at Jude. "We'll finish this later."

Jude blanked his comment and turned his attention to me. "Put these in that satchel," he said, undoing the buckles and shoving the food inside.

"Hurry up," tutted Raven. She helped Jude shove the last bag of crisps inside. "We need to get on that train."

The lights continued to flicker and a sense of doom seemed to fill the room. Gripping me by the shoulder, Ben marched me out onto the platform, and his other hand pulled Max out behind him.

I felt my mood fade as there was no sign of the train yet. I strained my eyes along the track but it just looked empty.

Max paced back and forth up the platform. "Where the hell is that train?"

In the distance, I could just make out the first creeping signs of fog as it slowly lingered along the empty track towards us. Ben had been right. The Cleaners would never give up.

"*Come on – come on,*" I urged, covering my eyes with both hands and peeking through my fingers. The wait was too much. I could feel myself getting jumpy – fidgety. Where was the fucking train? I looked back at the ticket office door, suddenly nervous that the Cleaners might come through it. I turned back towards the track and felt my heart leap. "Shit, that's them – look!" In the distance, five shadowy shapes emerged from out of the fog.

"Fuck, let's bail!" shouted Max, turning back to the door of the ticket office.

"No, wait," ordered Ben, pulling Max back. "The train is coming."

I looked back down the track, and out of the fog, two lights appeared just behind the Cleaners. I jumped up and down on the spot. A nervous agitation filled me. "Come on, come on," I begged. Surely a train could outrun the Cleaners?

The train sounded its horn as a warning to passengers that it was approaching the station. Or maybe the train driver had seen the five ghostly shapes moving along the track. I gasped as it passed through the Cleaners – sending the fog sprawling in all directions. Thick plumes of it swirled up and then got sucked back down under the carriages like a vacuum taking the Cleaners with it.

As the train pulled into the station, Raven was already hammering the doors with her fists. "Open the fucking doors!" she shrieked, peering down towards the driver's cab.

The cold morning air was suddenly filled

with the hiss of the doors sliding open. Spinning around, Raven snatched hold of me and dragged me through into the carriage. Max clambered in behind, followed by Jude and Ben.

"Head down to the front of the train – near the driver's cab," ordered Ben, checking one last time out the door. "Hurry."

"Come on," urged Raven, shoving Max along the narrow aisle. He bumped into me, sending me sprawling to the floor. "Get up – get up!" Raven continued to push and shove.

"Will you calm the fuck down?" shouted Jude, pulling Raven aside and helping me back on my feet.

"There's no time for calm when the devil's slaves are on your back," glared Raven, climbing over the seats so she could get in front.

"It makes no difference if you're at the front of the line or at the back," glared Ben. "If the Cleaners are on this train, they'll get you anyway."

"Well I'm gonna make sure I'm the last to go," hissed Raven, reaching the interconnecting door which led through to the next carriage. She pushed the button and the door slid open.

We burst through, all of us in a panic to keep as much distance between the Cleaners and us.

The sudden sight of four passengers sitting in the carriage seemed to slow us down. Raven stopped abruptly – unsure of the four commuters who stared up at our sudden flurry.

"Move on to the next carriage," Ben whispered, calmly edging his way to the front of the line.

"Hey, I'm first," snapped Raven, reaching out to grab Ben as he passed her.

Ben spun around, his blue eyes shadowed. He towered over Raven.

Pulling on her arm, I whispered, "Don't, Raven. Let him go." I recognised that dark look. Fearful that Quint was going to come back full-blast, I stepped in front of Raven. Ben faced front and continued down the aisle. "Don't get him angry. We don't want his Demon to take over."

"He should be at the back," glared Raven. "He's already got an evil spirit lodger living inside him!"

"Shut the fuck up, will ya? Just bloody move!" Jude stood waiting impatiently at the back.

One of the commuters tutted at his swearing. The man peered over his newspaper, obviously annoyed at all the noise and turmoil we were causing. "Do you mind not using that disgusting language in here? Otherwise I'll have to get the guard."

"Whatever!" spat Raven. She continued along the aisle past a man who was peeling an apple with a knife.

"Not exactly keeping a small profile here, are we?" whispered Max, looking at the floor, avoiding eye contact with the passengers.

"That's the last of my worries," I hushed, breathing a sigh of relief as the train pulled out from the station. Even though we were on the move, I wondered who else had boarded the train.

As I stepped inside the last carriage, I peered out through the window. There was no sign of any fog. Had we got away? Had we, just by the skin of our teeth, escaped the Cleaners again? I sat down by the window. I had a good view of the door leading back to the carriage we had just come from. If the Cleaners came through, at least I would be able to see them coming. I chewed nervously on my lower lip. An uncomfortable pang twisted and churned inside my stomach. I could feel my heart racing, an unnatural beat of mayhem and unrest. That horrible feeling of VA20 pulsed through my veins like it was pushing deeper inside me – fighting to take over. Anarchy swarmed within me. I tried to take deep breaths, tried to calm down the riot that was bursting through me. I looked down at my nails. They had got longer – thicker. I could almost see my fingers stretching just like Ben's had looked when Quint had overtaken him. Breathe – breathe. I needed to calm down. My eyes stared back at the door. How the hell was I going to calm down when there was every chance that the Cleaners were working their way through each carriage looking for us? But they might not be. That's what I had to keep thinking – keep telling myself. I stood up.

"Where ya going?" asked Jude.

"I'm just trying to relax." I paced up and down, stumbling slightly as the train rocked from side to side.

"Relax?" sneered Raven. "We're not going on holiday, ya know."

Before I even knew what I was doing, I had a hold of Raven around her throat. My vine-like fingers slipped around her neck and I yanked her up off her seat. "Why don't you just shut that vile fucking mouth!" I slammed her back down onto the seat and continued to hold her tight around the throat.

"Kassidy, Kassidy, can you hear me?" Jude's voice sounded off in my ear. "Let go of Raven!" He pulled on my fingers, trying to release the grip I had on her.

I stared down into Raven's hazy red eyes. Her black, twisted nails dug into my flesh. "Get off," she spluttered, reaching up with one hand and wrenching down on my hair.

What the hell was happening to me? I felt so confused, so angry. I could hear Max shouting for me to stop and Jude trying to prise my fingers from Raven. Then all of a sudden, two strong hands wrapped themselves around me and pulled me away like I was as light as air.

Raven shot up from the position I had held her in. She leered out from under her greasy hair. "She's fucking crazy! There must be a Demon in her already."

"Of course there is," Ben whispered, still holding me tight. "There's six inside her – six in you – in all of you. That's what VA20 is."

CHAPTER SIX

I'm sorry," I whispered, not really directing my comment at anyone in particular. "I just felt really anxious and then angry – really angry. I don't know what happened." I looked at Raven's stormy face. She was fucked off. Seething, in fact.

"Hey, it's all right," smiled Jude, patting my knee as he sat opposite me. "We all feel like doing that to Raven."

"Fuck you," spat Raven, turning her back to us. She folded her arms across her chest and stared quietly out the window.

"I don't like this crap in my veins," I said. "I want it out of me. It's like it takes over. When I get anxious or angry it seems to get stronger. I've never attacked anyone before – only since this shit was injected into me." I held up my arms and rolled back the sleeves of my top. "Just look at it. It's like a disease." I stared up at Ben, who stood beside my seat in the aisle. "You did this! This is your fault."

Ben let out a deep sigh and nodded his head slowly. "If I could change the past, then I would. But I can't. All I can do is help you get to Doctor Langstone – even though I believe it will be a wasted journey."

"Do you think we got away from the Cleaners?" asked Max, peering out the window.

"Fuck knows," answered Jude, leaning over and opening up Father Williams' satchel. He pulled out some crisps and settled back in his seat. "Maybe the good doctor here can answer that." He tipped up his crisp packet and emptied half the bag into his mouth.

"You know what the Cleaners are like," said Max, staring at Ben, "Do you think they've gone?"

"I have no control over the Cleaners. They do what Doctor Middleton asks them to do – for now, anyway," said Ben. "All they want is a body to live in. They will go to whoever gains sufficient bodies that will be strong enough to withstand them. So a Demon who has you four will be an attraction to the Cleaners but..." He trailed off.

"But what?" I pushed.

"You're not enough," Ben stared down at me. "More bodies are needed."

"How many more?" asked Max.

"I thought it was just four... but... I don't know now... something inside me... I feel like... I don't know," Ben shook his head. "My brain is so full of shit... it's so dark in there. I have my thoughts, my memories, well sometimes, but I've got this other thing living inside me... his thoughts eat away at me – infect me. He blocks out stuff he doesn't want me to know. Makes me forget myself – takes away my identity."

"Is there no way you can get rid of it?" asked Max, "Can't we take you to a priest or Bishop so they can perform an exorcism? If we got it out of you, then you could help us more – help us get this drug out of our veins."

"Don't you think I've already tried that?" snapped Ben. "I went to see a Father Peter. I met him in the grounds of Cruor Pharma one morning. I was feeling strong that day, I had more control over the Demon, so I asked this priest if he could help me."

"What happened?" I asked, remembering what the Bishop had told us about the priests he had sent to the chapel and what had become of Father Peter.

"The priest was shit scared of me, he stood there like a quivering wreck, clutching his rosary beads in his hands."

"What did you do?" I whispered, fearing that it had been Ben who had finished off Father Peter at the railway station.

"What did *I* do?" Ben almost laughed. "I didn't do anything, my Demon decided to make an appearance, and the last I remember of Father

Peter was him running away down Strangers Hill reciting some prayer over and over again."

"So it wasn't you who pushed him in front of that train?" I asked, staring into Ben's eyes, trying to see any sign that he was lying.

"That would have been the Cleaners, but I'm sure my Demon played a part in that." Ben crouched down so he could see out of the window. "So, there is no getting the Demon out of me, and even if it were possible… I still wouldn't be of any help. This body of mine only exists while the Demon is in me. No Demon – no more Ben. As much as I long for that day to come, for now, I'm here and I will try my best to keep you safe."

"You want to die?" I asked, my heart sagging.

"Life isn't worth living when you're not *really* living, Kassidy," whispered Ben. "There's no peace for me – probably won't be any peace when this Demon finally gives me up either. I'm hell-bound – alive or dead with what I've been a part of. There's no place in heaven for me."

"My heart bleeds for you," Jude cut in. "What a load of emotional bullshit! Don't fall for this crap. It's just another way of getting around you. Can't you see he's playing you? The Demon wants you to trust him – to feel sorry for him."

"Jude, it's not Ben's fault..." I began.

"Yes, it is! Don't forget who pushed that needle into you... don't forget..."

Ben stood up and leant over Jude. His eyes had darkened a little. "Are you to be trusted? Are you..."

The train suddenly swayed and jolted. The overhead lights flickered. The morning glow vanished as the train entered a tunnel.

"It's okay, just a tunnel," Jude said, staring out of the window.

The carriage had become gloomy. I looked up at Ben but it was too dark to see the colour of his eyes.

"Ben, are you still with us?" I asked, hoping Quint wouldn't be the one to answer.

"I'm still here," whispered Ben, taking my hand and giving it a reassuring squeeze.

I peered down the carriage. It was like a dark tunnel within a tunnel. The train rocked left and right as the wheels clacked over the rails. The door to the next carriage suddenly slid open making me jump. I perched on the edge of my seat. Watching. Waiting. There was nothing there. I could just about see into the first half of the next carriage. I could see the gloomy shapes of the four passengers still sitting on their seats. Feeling a little more relaxed that everything seemed to be all right, I settled back into my seat and watched the tunnel walls go by. As I looked out the window, I caught sight of Raven's reflection. She was staring at me. I shuddered. It reminded me of how she had been on Ward 2. I twisted round in my seat and faced her. "Why are you staring at me?"

Her gloomy face came nearer as she shifted across to the seat next to her. "Can't you feel it?" She looked over her shoulder down the carriage towards the open door.

I swallowed hard as I followed her gaze. "Feel what?" I couldn't see anything – couldn't hear anything other than the echo of the train passing through the tunnel.

"The train is slowing," she muttered, still staring at me. "Why is it slowing down?"

"Probably some kind of speed restriction when the train passes through a tunnel." Jude leant forward and shoved his hand into the satchel. I could feel him rummaging through the crisps. He pulled his hand out clutching a chocolate bar. "Want some?" He waved it in front of my face.

"No, thanks," I muttered, trying to concentrate on the speed of the train. I turned to Max. "It's slowing down a lot, don't you think?"

Before Max could answer, a muffled voice

sounded from over a speaker system. The train came to a juddering halt.

"Ladies and Gentlemen, there appears to be something blocking the track up ahead. Please stay seated while I check it out. Thank you for your patience."

The carriage fell silent. The lights flickered dimly, casting an eerie, flimsy glow. I stood up. "I don't like this. Something's wrong." I looked at Ben. He was still standing in the aisle. I could tell by the grim look across his face that he felt the same.

"Something vile is coming," whispered Raven. "I can sense it." She stood up.

"It's called Raven," sniggered Jude, popping the last bit of chocolate into his mouth.

I kicked him in the leg. "Stop it! This isn't the time for jokes."

"I can't see anything outside. Just the tunnel walls," whispered Max. He had his face and hands pressed up against the window.

"Who says it's something outside?" muttered Raven as she peered down into the next carriage.

CHAPTER SEVEN

We followed Raven's gaze. The aisle up ahead leading through into the next carriage was empty, except for the four passengers who had been seated in there when we had first got on. No shadowy figures or anything had appeared out of the dimly lit train.

Max pulled open the small pane of glass across the top of the main window. He pressed the side of his face up against it and listened. The *drip-drip* sound of water echoed in the tunnel. Nothing else could be heard apart from the heavy breathing coming from us.

"I think we should get off this train," I whispered. My legs and arms felt shaky. That horrible feeling in my stomach had returned.

"Sit down and chill," said Jude, pulling on my wrist. "You're just feeling paranoid – that's all. Quite understandable after what we've been through. You heard what the driver said – the track has something on it – he'll be back in a minute and then we'll be off again."

I looked at the end of the carriage and wished there were windows into the driver's cab so I could see what it was the driver had spotted on the tracks.

"What if it's the Cleaners out there?" whispered Raven. She stood with her arms wrapped around her.

"Why the fuck would the Cleaners be out there? Playing chicken on the railway tracks now are they?" scoffed Jude. "If the Cleaners were here then they'd be inside with us."

I began to look around the carriage. Where were the exits? I felt sick when I realised there were no doors except for the one out in the vestibule in-between this carriage and the next. That only left the door into the driver's cab but everyone knew that always stayed locked.

"It's okay," said Max, coming away from the window, "Listen, I can hear the driver's footsteps. He must be coming back to the train."

I went to the window. Sure enough, I could hear the crunch of boots walking slowly back toward the train. Still, it didn't lift that feeling that something wasn't right. I looked at Ben. "I want to get off. This doesn't feel safe."

"Me too," whispered Raven. "The dead are coming – they want to take us."

"Led by the Grim Reaper himself, eh Raven?" said Jude, his tone sarcastic.

"We need to stay on this train if we're ever

to get to Doctor Langstone," said Ben. "If we get off now, it could take us a while to get there."

"I don't care," I said. "Look where we're sitting. It's a dead end. The only door behind me is the one into the driver's cab but that won't help us if something comes down that aisle from the carriage up ahead. The driver's cab will be locked. We're trapped."

"Let's move to the next carriage then," said Ben. "At least in there we can exit either end. I know what you feel, Kassidy. I feel it too. But let's hold off on here as long as we can. We don't want to be getting off into this tunnel in the pitch black and get run down by another train."

"I'd rather take my chances with another train than with the Cleaners," I said, pulling Father Williams' rosary beads out from under my top.

"Come on," whispered Ben, holding out his hand for me to take. "I'll keep you safe."

"Of course you will," glared Jude. "But who's gonna keep us safe from you?"

Ben didn't even acknowledge Jude. He continued to keep his eyes on me.

I looked up into his face. His skin had an eerie glow about it from the flickering lights above. The lower half was still shadowed by stubble but his blue eyes had a glimmer about them. Those lips of his could melt mine with one smouldering kiss. I took his hand, and the fragrance of his musty aftershave sweetened the fear I felt eating away at my insides.

"Can you keep me safe? Can you really keep away everything and everyone that's after me – after us?" I whispered. "Or do you have to be Quint to do that?"

I felt Ben flinch at my comment and immediately I regretted saying what I had. He must have felt insignificant. Like I was comparing his strength to that of Quint. "I didn't mean that like it sounded. I meant, do *you* have those powers – if that's what you call them – when Quint is silent? Can you hang from ceilings and open doors without Quint taking over your mind?"

"I don't know," shrugged Ben. His eyes had grown cold and he let go of my hand and turned away.

Cursing myself for coming across as being tactless, I looked at the others. "What do you all think? Should we stay on the train or get off?"

"Off," Raven grumbled from beneath her hair.

"Stay," answered Max. "But let's move to the next carriage." He stood up and squeezed past me.

"It's too dangerous to stay," argued Raven. "We're not alone on here."

"Stay!" Jude jumped up from his seat. "There's no sign of the Cleaners – just some dead animal on the tracks probably – that's all. If you want to get to Langstone's then travelling on the train is the quickest way to get there – not on foot."

I looked at Raven and shook my head. I couldn't help but feel that staying was the wrong move to make.

A loud bang had my heart leaping into my throat. I spun around. Was that the driver's door? Had he finally finished on the tracks? I waited with my breath held. If the train started moving then maybe I would feel more at peace with staying.

The carriage was suddenly filled with the sound of static coming from the loud speaker. I lingered in the aisle, waiting for the driver's voice to inform us that the train would be moving on. I looked at Raven. She remained frozen to the spot. The others waited at the end of the carriage. Still nothing from the driver. I walked slowly down the aisle towards the others. The static got louder. Something in the corner of my eye made me stop. I stared intently through the window to my right. Had I just imagined something swirl past the glass?

A reflection maybe? I paused. Nothing. No – there it was again. Just a flicker – just a wisp. A tendril of smoke. I swallowed hard. No – not smoke. Fog.

CHAPTER EIGHT

"Fog," I breathed, reaching the others. "There's fog out there." I pushed past Jude and Max. "Let's go, now!"

"Are you sure?" asked Max, crouching a little so he could peer out through the window.

"Yes I'm fucking sure!" I snapped, squeezing past Ben. I reached for the button to release the door but Ben snatched my arm and pulled it away.

"What are you doing?" I glared. "We need to get off this train."

Taking hold of me by my arms, he shunted me to the side and looked out through the window of the door. "I can't see any fog."

"Look, I don't give a shit whether you can see fog or not," I snapped. "I saw it, so I'm leaving."

"No, you're not," ordered Ben.

Without answering him, I reached out again for the button.

Ben grasped my wrist and yanked it away. "Until I see fog for myself, we all stay put. And besides, if they're out there, wouldn't you rather be in here?"

"No, I wouldn't, because while we'll stuck on a train that isn't moving, we're easier to get! At least out there we can run," I spat, trying to wrench my wrist from his grasp.

Ben turned to the others and said, "Have any of you ever tried to run on train tracks? In the pitch black through a tunnel?"

They shook their heads.

"You'll all have broken ankles before you even make the end of the tunnel – that's if you don't get mowed down by another train on the other track. It's too risky to be stumbling around out there." He turned back to face me. His cold look softened a little. "Now let's just go and sit down in the next carriage with the other passengers and try to stay calm. If the train doesn't start moving soon then we'll rethink our next step, okay?"

Max and Raven turned away. Jude hovered, his eyes lingered from me to Ben. I knew what he must be thinking. He didn't like leaving me alone with Ben, especially after what had happened that night at the Bishop's. He left with a glare spread over his face. I heard the door slide open as Jude entered the other carriage. I scowled up at Ben. "Why do you speak to me like I'm a schoolgirl? If I want to get off this train then I'm old enough to make that decision without your consent." I tried again to shake off his hands that still gripped my wrists. But Ben was too strong.

He pushed me gently up against the vestibule wall and leant against me. His lips brushed over my ear. "Because I'm in charge, and you invited me, remember?"

I turned my head and glanced into Ben's face. His eyes wavered with ripples of black. He pushed his muscular body against me. He felt muggy – scorching. His fiery lips pressed fiercely against mine. His tongue hot like a flame licking from a furnace. I tried to push him away.

"Don't pretend you don't want me, Kassidy."

I could feel myself shudder from his touch. His body pressed up against mine made me feel like I was drowning in lava. Yet I wanted him. I needed to feel him. His body was like a magnet pulling me in. Small trickles of sweat ran down the side of my face. Hot fingers pushed down the insides of my jeans, snatching at the flesh on my arse. For a moment I was lost within a bubbling volcano. All fears of the Cleaners had melted away along with any rational thoughts I'd had before. I was sinking in temptation. Pleasure came first. I reached up and grabbed the sides of his face, pulling him towards my lips. I was hungry for him.

Quint ravenously covered my soft lips. "It's

been so long that I've felt like this," he breathed. "You bring out everything that a Demon has within him – everything bad yet it feels so good." His hands slipped out from my jeans and glided up my sides – his fingers teased under the fabric of my bra, rubbing my breasts.

My heart pounded in a frenzy as my flesh sizzled from his touch. My nipples responded to the stroke of his fingertips. I pushed my hands up under his shirt and let my hands slide over his tight muscles. My body shook. I was on a high. Nothing had ever made me feel like this. I was floating in indulgence. If this was a sin, then I wanted more.

"I never thought I would find the love I once had – so long ago – so many decades have past. But you – you bring out the devil in me," Quint whispered as he nipped my ear.

I stared up into his black eyes. They were like two fervent pools of tar, drenched with lust... with... desire... no. Sadness?

"Etta," Quint whispered. He was so close yet his mind had drifted far away – lost in a memory that halted his interest in me. His hands dropped away from under my top and grasped me by the face, tilting my head up so he could look upon me.

"Quint?" I hushed, suddenly unsure of what

was happening. What was going on inside that head of his?

Quint blinked, and the two pools of tar were replaced with crystal blue.

"Ben?" I gasped.

"No! We can't do this!" Ben pulled away from me like I'd stung him. He backed away, his body pressed against the door.

With a cold sweat now instead of that lustful heat that Quint had made me feel, I stepped towards Ben and whispered, "Why? Why can't you?" I didn't understand. I'd gone from high to low within seconds – up there one minute – slapped down the next. "You kissed me – you touched me. Now you're giving me the cold shoulder."

"That wasn't me! It was Quint!" snapped Ben. "I can't get involved with you, Kassidy. I'll end up killing you! Quint will kill you! He'll make me do it. I think I did it before... I... I think I killed someone I loved... I'm not sure... my memories have faded..." He turned away from me and stared out the window.

"Do you have any feelings for me at all?" I whispered, closing my eyes to the rejection I feared was coming.

"No!"

The reply was firm enough, yet he couldn't face me. A cold barricade had been put up and I knew I couldn't break it down. I let out a deep sigh and slumped against the wall. "I can't deal with this... two people in one... it's crazy. I have no feelings for you, so I guess that makes us even." I turned away. Rejection didn't feel so good.

CHAPTER NINE

I straightened up my clothes before entering the carriage. Jude, Max, and Raven had chosen to sit halfway along, just past one of the other passengers. The other three commuters were dotted along the left side, two reading newspapers and the other one listening to an iPod. I could hear, "Big Love" by Fleetwood Mac, playing rather loudly and I was surprised that no one had complained about the volume, although it did help to drown out the static that still hissed from the speakers. Taking the seat next to Max, I sat quietly listening to the music. I was in no mood to talk. Quint had left my brain sizzling and Ben had left me feeling cold. Who was Etta? Someone Quint had loved long ago? What had happened to her? I could only imagine the worst – it did involve Quint, after all. Did Demons really love? I had always imagined them to be evil through and through – not able to have true feelings for anything or anyone. Weren't they just creatures that manipulated and tempted us? Quint had already shown me how good he was at that. And then there was Ben. If Quint wasn't inside him, what would he be like? Would he still reject me? Would he make me feel like Quint had made me feel out in the vestibule? Would I ever get to find out? I felt my heart sink as I knew that Ben and Quint stayed as one. Without Quint, there would be no Ben. If we were to get rid of the Demons then I would lose both of them. I slumped back in my seat. I felt deflated. How could I ever have any kind of relationship with Ben? And wasn't I just being bloody stupid for even having such thoughts? What rational person would even consider getting involved with someone like Ben, or something like Quint? I tutted out loud.

"What's wrong with you? Lover-boy given you the cold shoulder?" mumbled Jude.

I felt my face flush as Max and Raven looked up at me. They seemed surprised by Jude's comment.

"He's not my lover-boy," I glared at Jude. "He's a cold bastard who obviously doesn't have feelings for anyone."

"That's why your tongue hangs out like a lovesick puppy every time Ben walks past, is it?" snapped Jude, leaning forward in his seat. "What was I the other night? A stand-in? Your second choice?"

"I was upset! I couldn't sleep!" I shouted.

"So you thought you'd kill time by jumping into bed with me?" spat Jude.

"It wasn't like that," I hissed. "You know it wasn't!" I sheepishly looked at Max and Raven, who were pretty much stuck in between Jude and me. What must they think of me? Jude was making me out to be some kind of slag, but it hadn't been like that. I'd been weak – messed up. I'd just wanted to sleep – to not be alone in all this shit.

"The devil's hands have already got a hold of you," glared Raven, "That's what they do! I might be next! I'm gonna keep my distance from Dr. Fletcher!"

Jude screwed his nose up at Raven. "I don't think you've got anything to be worried about." He rolled his eyes in disbelief at her comment.

"No one's got their hands on me," I snapped. "And no one ever will – *ever again*!" I made a point of directing that comment at Jude. Thank God I hadn't let it go any further with him. How many more mistakes was I going to make? It seemed that the moment I had stepped foot into Cruor Pharma was when I'd lost all sense of good judgment. Maybe I never had any in the first place? I looked at Max who gave me a reassuring smile. I hadn't made a mistake in befriending him. I half smiled back. Then standing up, I pulled the rest of the crisps and chocolate bars out of the satchel and threw them at Jude. "Here, gorge yourself on these, it's what makes you happy!"

I spun around and slumped myself down on another seat just behind them. I wanted to be by myself, only my eyes fell upon Ben. He sat a little further down the carriage. He stared at me. His gaze seemed to pierce right through me. I glared back at him, folded my arms across my chest, and lifted my feet up onto the opposite seat. Fucking men! Fucking Demons! I could feel my blood pumping again. I could sense the anger building up within me. I clenched my fists. I could quite easily knock every single guy out on this train. Smack them in the mouth and... No, I had to stop feeling like this. This anger was no good for me. I could feel it seeping through my veins like a poison. Think happy thoughts – that's what I needed. I racked my brain for some. Think – think. No matter how hard I tried to remember happy memories, I just came up with bad. Turning to face the window, I looked out upon the tunnel walls. Was this train ever gonna get moving again? Every second we spent sitting static allowed the Cleaners to get nearer. My concerns must have been playing in Raven's head as she suddenly stood up.

"We've waited long enough," she moaned. "Let's get off this train."

"Sit down!"

I jumped at the sudden outburst that had come from Ben. Only it wasn't him, it was Quint standing by the door. He looked so angry. Someone you wouldn't want to mess with.

"Don't argue with him, Raven," I heard Max whisper. He reached up and pulled on Raven's arm.

"But we're in danger just waiting here. They're coming – I know it -and we're just sitting here letting them catch up with us!"

The other passengers had started to get fidgety. Whether it was because of Quint yelling his orders, or Raven's sudden outcry that we were in danger, or maybe they were just getting pissed off with the train stuck in this goddamn tunnel. Whichever it was, I could hear them moaning to one another.

"I'm going to be late for my meeting," said the man who had been reading a newspaper. He shook the creased up pages about in frustration.

"I don't understand what all the delay is about, this train has never been late before," said a lady, dressed in a smart suit. "It doesn't help that we're stuck in this carriage with these people."

"Degenerates, that's what they are. Have you seen those black veins on that guy's arm? Drug takers – the lot of them I reckon. Best just to ignore them," hushed the guy holding the newspaper.

I shook my head. What an arsehole. If only they knew. One thing I had learnt since entering Cruor Pharma was to not judge a book by its cover – even the nice ones. You never knew what lay beneath its shiny, good-looking cover. I stared back at Quint. He stood at the end of the carriage, watching, making sure that we all stayed put. I could still hear Raven arguing her point that we should all leave.

The flickering lights started up again and I found myself, face pressed up against the window, looking for fog. The speakers hissed even louder. Why hadn't the train driver updated us? I pulled open the small window and tried to hear if there was any movement coming from outside within the tunnel. I cursed, unable to hear anything, what with Raven moaning, the static from the speakers, and the music playing from the iPod. It was impossible to make out any kind of noise from outside. Still, there was no fog. But I was sure I had seen some only a short while ago. Maybe I was just being paranoid?

As I went to shut the window, the lights went out – stuttering into nothingness.

CHAPTER TEN

I couldn't see a thing. I stumbled blindly, reaching out for the top of the seats, trying to find my way into the aisle. The static filled the black void I now staggered around in. The iPod blurted out through the breaks in the hissing and the sound of tripping feet thumped about.

"Max, are you there?" I called, trying to locate the others.

I felt a hand grasp my arm. I flinched. Unsure who it belonged to.

"It's me – Max." He squeezed my arm.

"Is everyone okay?" I asked, letting Max guide me down into a seat. It was like the blind leading the blind.

A sudden flash of light had me jumping in my seat. I let out a shaky sigh when I realised it was just the iPod that one of the passengers had been using. The silhouette of the owner sat quite casually, selecting another song, seemingly unscared of the dark carriage. But why would he be? He had no idea of what could be coming.

The driver's voice suddenly erupted from the speakers.

"There will be no service today. Stay seated

and wait for me to come and get you – get you – get you – get..." The voice echoed through the hiss of static and then fell silent.

"What the fuck?" I heard Jude say. "I think it's time we vacated, don't you?"

A shadow appeared to loom over us as we sat in our seats. It came out of the dark and leant over me.

"Get up. We're leaving." It was Ben's voice but, unable to see, I wasn't sure if it was Quint.

"Told you!" I whispered. "We should have left sooner. You, of all people, know what the Cleaners are like."

"This isn't the Cleaners," he said. "This is something else."

"What?" I asked. What could be worse than the Cleaners? What had Ben or Quint seen, if not the Cleaners, that had made him want to leave the train? "Is it the police?" I feared them in a different way. I hadn't liked the look of Inspector Cropper when I had been hiding in the back of the Cruor Pharma van. I knew he was bent and worked alongside Doctor Middleton, covering up the horrors of what went on in that hospital on top of Strangers Hill. I felt sure that if we all posed a risk of outing what Cropper had been a part of, then he wouldn't hesitate to dispose of us, regardless of

Middleton wanting us taken back to Cruor Pharma.

"No, it's not the police... I don't know what it is... but I think we should go."

As I stood up, the whole carriage seemed to shake on its wheels. As it shunted into the carriage behind, an awful crunch of metal filled the air. The groan of wheels forcibly being pushed over the tracks had my heart racing. I fell back down.

"What the hell did that?" whispered Max. "Has Middleton created some kind of giant monster? It must be pretty big to move train carriages."

"Where I come from, you don't need to be big to be powerful," said Quint. "Now get up."

Standing up on shaky legs, I blindly reached out for something to hold – something that would help me find the way out. The lights suddenly sprang back on, but not fully. They blinked on and off like lights at a rave. My eyes tried to adjust to the surroundings in the carriage. Stopping dead in my tracks, I stared at the other passengers. None of them had moved. It was like they were unaware that the train had even smacked into the other carriage. The two who had been reading newspapers still sat with them held up in front of their faces. The guy with the iPod was leant forward staring at the screen. I looked at the commuter who was seated behind us, the one who had been peeling an apple. His face was turned away, peering out through the window. Hadn't they heard the train driver's announcement? Didn't they think it odd? Why weren't they even complaining? Something felt very wrong here. I turned to Raven. She was still sitting in her seat, only, she rocked back and forth. Her greasy hair hung over her face as she peered up at me. I gasped and nearly stumbled over. Her eyes had that red, misty look about them. The black veins, which ran up her neck, were pulsing, pushing through under her skin like a thick worm wriggling through dirt.

"Don't you leave me," she hissed, "They're coming and we have to get out. We're not ready, I'm not ready yet..." She clawed at the skin on her face and continued to rock forward.

The lights persisted to flash on and off. I reached down and took hold of Raven's arm. As scary as she appeared, I knew it was the VA20 that seemed to plague her. She continued to stay rooted to the spot. I looked up for the others. They had already reached the end of the carriage. "Come on, Raven," I pleaded. "I'm trying to help you."

"Kassidy, come on!" shouted Jude.

The carriage rocked again. I fell onto Raven. She grabbed a handful of my hair, twisting the strands around her palm like she was rolling up a ball of string. Reaching my roots, she yanked down hard.

I yelled out, trying to release the grip she had on me.

"You have to stay with me," she muttered. "We need to keep together."

"Raven, please!" I gasped, the pain in my scalp burning. "Please, I'm not leaving you, I'm trying to take you with me."

"I can feel it," spat Raven. "It's in me." She clawed at her neck with her free hand, her black fingernails ripping at the veins under her skin.

"It's VA20!" I shouted, managing to pull her fingers from my hair. "You have to fight it, don't let it take you over!" I pulled away from her and stood up.

My heart almost stopped when I looked down the carriage. The other passengers now sat staring up at me. Only there was no colour to their eyes. Their pupils had disappeared, leaving creamy, white balls in their sockets. Their mouths hung open, like they were waiting to be fed. My eyes skipped nervously from each passenger, then fell upon the end of the carriage where my heart sank, realising that Ben, Max, and Jude had disappeared from sight.

"I'm leaving, Raven," I whispered, not taking my eyes from the passengers. "I can't wait any longer." I took one last shot at pulling her up from her seat. She wobbled on her feet but made no more resistance to stay.

Taking a deep breath, I cautiously stepped forward. I didn't want to walk down the aisle in between the other passengers, but if I wanted to join the others, I had no choice. Should I just run for it? No, that would surely make them get up and make a grab for me. If I stayed calm then perhaps I could just get past them and they would stay seated. They seemed to be in some kind of trance.

Trying to stay focused on reaching the end of the carriage, I wondered where Ben and Max had disappeared to. I felt relieved to see that Jude was just inside the vestibule. I wanted to shout to him – to let him know that Raven and I could be in trouble, but I feared that would only kick-start the passengers into snatching us. Over the hiss of the static, I could hear a loud bang coming from within the vestibule. Maybe Ben and Max were trying to find a way out of the train.

What should have only been a few seconds' walk through the carriage felt more like forever. I took one step at a time. Raven followed close behind. I could hear her heavy breathing and she seemed to be mumbling to herself. I prayed silently that she wouldn't freak out as I tried to pass by the passengers. As I walked slowly by the guy who had been peering out through the window, he suddenly stood up and dropped his jacket to the floor. His chest was naked and he flung out his arm. My eyes widened as I saw a flick-knife clenched in his fist. I froze. Raven bumped into me.

He brought the knife down, hard into his chest. I heard the thud as the knife hit bone. Blood oozed as he pulled the knife back out. Then, holding the weapon with both hands he started to cut away at his skin. A series of bloody lines marked his flesh and he started to scream. I could feel myself shake. He was using the knife to write with. His chest was like a sheet of paper. I pushed back into Raven, too afraid to move forward.

The door to the vestibule slid open. The screaming man had alerted Jude, Max, and Ben that all was not well, but as they came running back into the carriage, the other passengers stood up and stepped into the aisle, blocking their way.

"Go the other way!" yelled Jude. I could just make out the top of his head, the rest of him hidden behind the passengers.

"Raven, you need to turn around," I whispered, my voice wavering. "We have to go out the other way." I flinched as the man with the knife started to swing it wildly around, the blade glinting on and off in the flickering overhead lights. His arm swung with such force, it was like he was lifting a heavy axe. The knife missed me by an inch and thudded into one of the seats.

"Look," whispered Raven, pointing at the man's chest.

"What?" My eyes widened as I realised that the bloody lines scratched out upon the man's skin spelt Doshia. Trickles of blood seeped from the letters and with each move the man made, the lines opened up wider, like fleshy slices cut into raw steak. "Move back." I elbowed Raven in the stomach, stepping on her toes as she tried to turn around. Regaining her balance, she suddenly stopped dead.

As I stepped backwards, the knife sliced through the air just in front of my face. It glided so fast it was like a bolt of lightning.

"You need to keep moving!" I screamed at Raven. "Or I'm gonna end up with my face sliced open!" The gap between me and the man was getting slimmer. I knew that his next attempt with the knife would cut me.

"I can't," shouted Raven, "It's blocked!"

Shooting a look over my shoulder, I realised we were trapped. There were more passengers who had stepped into this carriage from the one adjacent to ours. They all wore the same empty, white-eyeball look - mouths hung open.

I turned back just as the knife rained down. I darted to my left and jumped up onto one of the seats. With Raven's back to the knife, I knew the man was going to aim for her. As he swung his arm up, I threw myself onto his back. The man staggered to and fro like a tightrope walker threatening to fall. We weren't going to simply escape from this train. Not now. With VA20 raging through my veins, the anger spurned me on. We were going to have to fight our way out.

CHAPTER ELEVEN

My arms clung around the man's throat. His skin was hot and slippery. I wrapped both legs about him and swayed back, hoping to throw him off balance and bring him down to the floor. His arms swung widely at Raven, the knife slashed in all directions as if hoping by chance it might hit a target.

The passengers in front of Raven began to push down the aisle, forcing us back along the carriage to where the other commuters blocked Jude, Max, and Ben. We were trapped in the middle. Over the hiss from the speakers, I could hear Jude shouting at Max, seats being clambered over, and bodies tumbling about.

Knowing that if I didn't do something fast, Raven, sandwiched in the middle, would soon have a knife in her back.

I slapped the palms of my hands across the man's face, and gritting my teeth, I shoved my black, twisted nails into his eyes. I felt them pop as the nails pierced through. My stomach lurched. Wet, mushy clots splattered onto my hands like raw egg. It clung between my fingers in a stringy slush. Still, it didn't stop the shiny blade from slashing wildly towards Raven.

"I need some fucking help here!" I screamed, hoping that Quint might show himself. When I didn't get an answer, I yelled at Raven. "Kick out the window! The one in the middle... it's an emergency exit."

Raven darted in between the seats and climbed up and over. She kicked at the glass with the heel of her foot. "These freaking shoes," she screamed. "I can't do it!"

The carriage suddenly shunted back again. The loud clang of metal thundered through the train. I held onto the man's neck as tightly as I could. The sudden movement of the carriage had him toppling down, with me wedged underneath him. I caught sight of the wet mess dribbling down the side of his face where it leaked from his burst eyeball. It had dripped down onto his chest and mixed with the blood running from the slashes he had cut. He held the knife up and stabbed it down just above his shoulder. It missed me – just. Snatching hold of his wrist as he brought it down again, the sharp point glinted just above my face. The other passengers crowded the aisle in front of us. Their empty eyes lacked any kind of emotion. They were like brain-dead spectators. The carriage seemed to tip slightly to the left. I used its momentum to haul the man off me. Clambering to my feet, and with all the strength I had, I pulled him up by his hair, running at the window – him as a barricade. His body hit the glass. Dragging him back, I ran again. Face-first, he smashed into the window. The glass buckled slightly.

"Help me," I panted at Raven.

She jumped off the chair. Snatching a handful of the man's hair, and with the other hand firmly placed against his bare back, we ran full-force, smacking into the window. The glass cracked and fell out into the tunnel. We both looked at each other, and as if thinking the same, we both yelled, "Throw him out!"

Pulling him back and then charging again, the man hit the side of the carriage and toppled out into the dark. The sound of his knife hitting the track clattered through the tunnel.

Trying to catch my breath, I turned around. The passengers had moved forward. My eyes quickly checked their hands and I was relieved to see no more knives. Still, I didn't think I had enough strength left in me to fight my way through this lot. As I contemplated escaping out through the broken window, the passengers were suddenly knocked aside like skittles. They smacked up, hitting the roof. Some flew so hard that they became embedded into the side of the carriage walls. I stared in disbelief at how their bodies were thrown so easily like they were made of tissue.

Quint strolled down the aisle. His black eyes shone in the flashes of light. His stubbly jaw flexed, a glare spread across his face. As he stared at each passenger, one by one, the awful sound of bones splitting and snapping had me screwing my eyes shut tight. I cringed as their necks broke. Opening my eyes when the noise had stopped, I was met with the grim picture of bodies – their heads hanging limply on scrawny, twisted necks, embedded into the punctured metal of the walls.

"About time!" hissed Raven, glaring at Quint.

In a blink of an eye, Raven was dangling in the air, her legs kicking out as she clawed at her throat. She thrashed about, gasping as an unseen pressure was applied to her neck.

"You want to join the passengers?" grinned Quint, his eyes not leaving Raven.

"Stop it!" I yelled, pulling on Quint's arm. "Put her down!"

He laughed. "I'm not holding her." He held up his empty hands as if to prove it wasn't him.

"Yes, you are... somehow," I snapped. "Do it... you're gonna kill her!"

Raven's feet touched ground. She fell to her knees, gasping for breath.

I glared at Jude and Max, who just stood there. "Thanks for the help!"

"You invited him, remember?" snapped Jude.

I ignored his sarcastic comment and helped Raven to her feet. She glared out from under her hair at Quint but didn't say anything.

"Now what?" asked Max, looking over his shoulder. "What do we do now?"

"We get out of this train and follow the track out of the tunnel," I said. "Quint may have killed all these people, but whatever got under their skin is probably still here."

"What makes you say that?" asked Jude, brushing dirt and dust from the knees of his black trousers.

"The guy swinging his knife cut a name into his chest – Doshia. You remember Doshia, don't you?" I asked, grim thoughts of what had happened to Hannah creeping into my head.

"Doshia killed Hannah," whispered Max, his eyes nervously darting about the carriage. "He's one of the Demons that the Bishop mentioned."

"One of your lot," sneered Jude, his eyes narrowed as he glared at Quint.

"We should go," said Quint, his voice no longer menacing but softer – concerned even.

His expression made my stomach start to churn. I knew how strong Quint was, I had seen it with my own eyes. How he could kill someone without even having to touch them. So why the concern over Doshia?

"Is there something you're not telling us about this Demon?" I asked. "Is there something different about him?"

"Doshia has been missing for years," said Quint. "He has the ability to leave his host for long periods of time yet still keep the body living. He can multiply himself amongst human bodies, like you've just seen for yourself." Quint stared up at the lifeless passengers implanted into the carriage walls. "Doshia didn't have the patience to wait for Trabek to come up with human bodies compatible to hold the Cleaners. It was thought that he had just disappeared – content with wrecking human lives, whoever had the misfortune of crossing his path. But... it seems he has come back... back for you lot, I imagine."

"So Trabek is Doctor Middleton, and you – Ben, you're Quint... or is that the other way round? Who else was there?" mumbled Max, looking lost.

"Eras," I said, staring at Quint. "Whose body

does Eras live in?" I had already seen Eras, only he hadn't been in a body. He had been like a shadow gliding across the floor at the Bishop's house.

Quint's eyes seemed to light up. "Eras lives within Middleton's son... he isn't really a son of Trabek, it just so happened that when Doctor Middleton opened up our coffins – our prisons – his son was there. Eras took on the role of..."

"Look, we don't have time to be standing here listening to a history of Demons," moaned Jude. He had been leaning out the broken window, staring into the tunnel. "If this Doshia is on our backs, then we need to be going."

Just the name – Doshia, sent shivers up my back. I couldn't rid my head of what he had done to Hannah – what he had made her do. If he could get inside me... then... I didn't want to think about it. I began to wonder if it was ever going to be possible to reach Doctor Langstone with so many Demons and people after us. There was also the added danger of lone Demons wandering about who would love to live within us.

I headed for the broken window. At least we would no longer be trapped in the train. But peering out into the dark tunnel didn't make me feel any better.

CHAPTER TWELVE

We dropped from the train window, into the tunnel. Our feet crunched over the broken glass as we landed with a thud. It was cold and damp. I shivered as a drop of water from the roof of the tunnel splashed down onto my face. I peered along the side of the train. The last carriage was a little way off in the distance, its lights spluttered on and off like the rest of the train, but looking beyond it, I couldn't see the entrance into the tunnel. As I checked the other way, I realised that we must be right in the middle as I could see no sign of daylight. If it wasn't for the train lights, we would be in pitch-black.

"I don't like it out here," mumbled Raven. "It's creepy."

"You can always stay with the other passengers," said Jude, taking Raven's arm and pulling her in close to the train. "Stay off the other track, you never know when another train is gonna come along."

"Didn't know you cared," mumbled Raven, surprised by his thoughtfulness.

"I don't," said Jude. "I just don't want bits of your twisted-up body splattered over me."

My foot caught something loose on the track, it clattered across the ground, echoing through the tunnel. I bent down and realised it was the knife that had nearly ended up in me and Raven. I stood up quickly and strained my eyes in the dark for the body of the knife-wielding man. Feeling sick in my stomach when it was obvious that the guy must still be somewhere in the tunnel, I turned to Quint.

"Quint, the man who tried to stab me and Raven, is still in here – his body has gone," I whispered, peering through the dark, expecting to see the man jump out at us from the shadows.

"Best we get going then, and it's Ben – not Quint."

I stared up into his face, catching a glimpse of blue eyes in the flickering train lights. "Sorry," I whispered, hearing an annoyance in his voice. "You change from one to another so quickly – it's hard to keep up – especially in the dark. I can't see your eyes too good."

"Great!" hissed Raven, reaching down and picking up the knife. "Now we've got to watch out for that devil-guy leaping out at us. He could be anywhere!"

"Let's go back the way we came," said Jude. "We have no idea how long this tunnel stretches for – it could go on for a lot longer than the way we came in."

"No!" snapped Raven, stepping in front of Jude. "We have to keep moving forward – we should never go back. Those Cleaners are following us – if we go back then we'll end up walking straight into them."

"I agree," said Max, rubbing his arms with his hands, trying to keep warm. "Going back just delays our journey to Langstone's place. I want to find my brother and I want to get this drug out of me. I don't like the way it makes me feel."

"But we could get out of this tunnel quicker if we just go back the way we came in," persisted Jude. "If we go the way you want then we might be stuck in here for ages."

"I'm not going back that way!" snapped Raven. "You go if you want to, but I'm going with Max – and Kassidy." She took hold of my arm like she'd already made the decision for me.

"Let's just think about this for a minute," said Jude, his voice sounded impatient.

"We don't have time for a debate," said Ben. "You have everything you don't want following you and many more that will cross your path on your way. I know what the Cleaners do. I know how they work. When they catch up with you, they'll take over your bodies – your brains – everything. And before you know it, you'll be back inside Cruor Pharma, only your minds will no longer be yours. If Doshia gets..."

A noise suddenly echoed through the tunnel, stopping Ben in his tracks. It sounded like dragging footsteps shuffling over loose stones. It came from one of the last two carriages.

"What was that?" whispered Raven, still clinging to my arm.

"Rats?" said Jude. "This tunnel must be full of them."

"Bloody big rats," hushed Max, peering into the dark, the shuffling getting nearer.

"I'm going!" Raven said. "Come on." She pulled on my arm and grabbed Max.

Not needing to be persuaded, I turned away and followed close behind Raven. My heart thumped loudly in my chest. I looked over my shoulder and was thankful to see Ben and Jude walking behind me. I didn't want our group to split up, but more so, I didn't want to be the one at the back of the line.

As we reached the carriage we had originally sat in, the shuffling noise from behind seemed to now be coming from a different direction. But the echoes within the tunnel from our feet trudging over the tracks made it difficult to pinpoint where it was coming from. I wanted to run. I wanted to get out of the dark and into the light. I knew that a sunny day would offer me no protection from the evils that hunted us, but the dark gave us nothing but a disadvantage.

"Come on! Hurry up!" Raven looked over her shoulder. I could just make out through the dark her face etched with worry – her voice full of urgency.

I stumbled along the track, using my right hand to slide along the side of the train to help me keep my balance. Every couple of seconds, I peered back over my shoulder. Ben and Jude walked in silence, the dark behind them seemed to be chasing close behind – waiting to swallow them up. I shuddered as more drips of water fell upon my face. The train windows almost seemed to beg me to look at them with the lights spluttering on, then fading into dark. I tried not to stare up at them – afraid that a face would suddenly appear, pressed up at the glass. I wanted to tell myself to not be so stupid but I couldn't even console myself with that thought. I knew what horrors existed. I could never ever kid myself again that paranormal things were nothing but stories, films, and books. It was real – all of it, I believed.

Lost in my thoughts, my eyes checking each window as I passed by, I suddenly felt something snatch at my ankle. As I fell forward, I watched Max tumble down in front of me – then Raven. I gasped at the sight of a hand stretching out from underneath the train. It clawed at the air like bony spider legs as it tried to grab hold of my other ankle. I kicked out with my free leg, but the hand caught me. With both legs now held firmly, I twisted over onto my front and grasped at the other track. The hands pulled down tighter. I clung on to the running rail. I could feel my body shunt over the cold ground as the hands tried to drag me under the train. My fingers started to slip from the metal rail.

"No – no!" I gasped. "You're not taking me under that train!" With the will to stay alive, I took one hand off the rail and flung my arm forward as far as I could. My fingers blindly reached for the furthest rail. I propelled my body forward – snatching at the cold metal. The hands wouldn't let go. Instead they came with me. Shifting further and further up my body. I could feel a dead weight lying across the backs of my legs. Looking to my left, I could see Ben and Jude pinned over the tracks. They were held down by several people, only they weren't people anymore. They were just like the passengers on the train. Empty stares with mouths hung open. They must have come from the carriages further down. I could hear Raven screaming and Max shouting. The silent tunnel was now filled with the horrific sounds of a struggle. The body on top of me dragged itself further up. I could feel it breathing in my ear. I didn't want to turn my head. I didn't want to see its face so close up.

A male voice breathed into my ear. "Did Daddy not love you…?"

I shivered. Not only from his breath tingling down my neck like tiny needles, but the mention of my father. I turned my head. Cloudy white eyeballs glared from out the dark at me. "What did you say?"

"Doshia is waiting… he wants you…" The man lifted his head slightly and seemed to be staring at Ben – or was it Jude? With nothing but the whites of his eyes showing, it was hard to tell.

I tried to shift my body from underneath the man, but everywhere I moved – he moved with me. It was like our bodies had become attached. "Who is Doshia?" I asked, trying to wriggle free.

The man's empty gaze came closer. He pushed his face into mine. His cold hands slipped up my arms and latched tightly around my wrists, pressing them hard into the running rail. Instead of answering me, he lay on top of my body and laughed.

"Please… let me go…" I panted, feeling the air from my lungs being crushed out by the weight of the man. He continued to laugh. "If Doshia wants me… then why hasn't he taken me yet?"

The man laughed again, his body vibrated against me. "Because… I… need… more…"

I took a deep breath. I couldn't just lie here, I had to try again to move this man from off me. Holding tight on the tracks, I pulled with all my strength. I slipped out just a little from underneath him. The top half of my body was now lying over the tracks. With a little freedom, I twisted myself over. I could now see Max and Raven. A passenger had crawled up over Max, but Raven had managed to escape from underneath the woman who had held her down. I saw a flash of something glinting in the darkness – the knife that she had picked up from off the tracks. Raven swung it down into the woman's chest. Over and over again. With each stab came a panicked yell from Raven's lips. I continued to struggle with the man on top of me. The rails dug into my back. I lay at such an awkward angle it was impossible to shift the man – his weight crushed me. I looked right again. I couldn't see Ben or Jude for the heap of bodies that had piled themselves on top of them.

"Raven!" I yelled. "Help me!" I slapped the palms of my hands across the man's face as he leant over me, his mouth still hung open – dribble splattered my cheek in a thick slush and ran into the corner of my mouth. I shook my head and spat it out. He continued to laugh like a crazy person who had escaped from some mental asylum.

"Get... the fuck off... me...!" I shouted, grabbing a handful of his hair and pulling his head away from over mine. "Get..." I stopped yelling. Another noise sounded in my left ear. What was that? With all the other noises going on inside the tunnel, it was hard to tell. Was it a humming sound? No, maybe hissing? Both? I slapped the man's face away as he lunged at me again. The sound of hissing was still there, only this time, I could feel a mild vibration under me. I looked to my left. The tunnel was like a black hole – never-ending. The vibration was stronger. I felt suddenly sick. I knew what was coming down the tunnel. Pinned to the track, I knew I had to get off and warn the others.

CHAPTER THIRTEEN

The sudden realisation that a train would soon be passing through this tunnel had me fighting for my life. It spurned me on. I heaved and bucked my body. The weight of the man still crushed me to the tracks. Using my fists, I punched them into the sides of his face. His head just wobbled like it was attached to a spring.

"Train!" I yelled. "TRAIN!" I had no idea if the others had heard my cry. I looked down the tunnel. It was still pitch black. No sign of the train lights yet. I turned my attention back to the man on top of me. He still lay there laughing. I smacked my fist right into the centre of his face. Again, he still came back at me with his open mouth, dribble seeping down his chin. I tried to move my legs. They were stuck. I flung my arms around his fat body – trying to roll us both over. It was useless. I could barely move my hips. Where had all that strength gone that I'd had when fighting the man with the knife back in the train carriage? Where was Quint? Why hadn't he surfaced – taken over Ben? I pulled out the rosary beads from under my top. The silver cross glinted in the dark of the tunnel. I held it up – jabbing it at the man's face.

Nothing! No reaction whatsoever. I screamed out in frustration. What did I have to do to move this lump of a man from me? My heart beat so hard that it matched the vibrations coming from the tracks. The hiss had got louder. Another quick glance down the tunnel. Still no train lights but I knew it wouldn't be much longer.

"There's a fucking train coming!" I spat at the man. "Do you want to fucking die?" I snatched hold of his face. My nails sliced into his skin as I raked them down. I did it again. And again. In desperation, I stabbed them into his face. Pulled them out. Stabbed them through again. Blood gushed out and ran down his face. He looked like he'd had a cheese grater rubbed up and down his skin. It made no difference. I looked over at Raven. She was still stabbing at the woman. In-out, in-out, the blade came down, over and over again. At least she was off the tracks. Max tumbled over with one of the passengers. His head lay precariously over the rail. He kept glancing to his left. He knew what I knew – what was going to be running over his head if he lost the struggle.

The sounds of fighting and tussling were suddenly dispersed – overtaken by the train horn. A thunderous rumble echoed all about me. As I lay trapped, tears brimming in my eyes from fear, my hands grazed across the ballast. Instinctively, my fingers curled around one large rock. I lifted my arms. Both hands took hold of it. Adrenaline pumped through me – or was it VA20? A surge of strength brought down the rock. I heard a crack. It wasn't enough to knock the man out. I brought it up again. Smashed it down. The man's heavy body gave way, just a little. Enough though to gain the upper-hand. I shunted to the left and smashed the rock into the side of the man's head. My legs came free. I scrambled to my feet. The man snatched at my ankle. I booted him right in the face. "Have some of that!" I screamed. Then spinning around, I ran to where Max lay across the tracks. His blonde hair fanned out over the rail, his head dangerously in line for the train wheels. Yanking hold of the passenger who held him down, I snatched the knife from Raven and rammed it through the passenger's neck. It was all Max needed to roll out from beneath his prison. He jumped from the tracks to safety.

"Help me!" I screamed, shoving the passenger onto the tracks and running to the pile of bodies that seemed to swarm over Jude and Ben in a heap.

"Leave them!" Raven shouted, grasping my arm. "There's no time. Look!"

Her head turned in the direction of two small lights at the end of the tunnel. The train was almost upon us.

"No! We have to help them!" I screamed. I shook her hand from off me. "Max. Please!" I ran along the side of the track. Reaching down, I pulled the first body off. My heart raced with VA20. Its strength thrust around my insides. I glanced up at the oncoming train. The tunnel filled with a roar. The train horn sounded again. So many bodies — too many to lift in time. I screamed out again. Panic forced me on.

"Get off the tracks!" Raven yelled at me. She threw her arms about my neck and tried to pull me away.

Swinging around, I knocked her clean over. She hit the side of the train we had travelled on, falling to her arse — momentarily stunned.

I turned back to the bodies. Max was franticly trying to lift them.

"We're not gonna make it!" he shouted, peering up at the train. It roared down the tunnel toward us.

I could feel the tears sting my eyes as they bubbled up and trickled down over my face. "Ben! Jude!" I screamed. I stared at the heap. I knew we were too late. I knew I was gonna die trying. I kicked out at the bodies. The frustration and fear pumping through me suddenly seemed to surge to such a point, that I thought VA20 was finally going to kill me. I staggered forward, swaying over the heap of passengers. My eyes hazed over, my vision suddenly seeing everything in red. "Move! Move!" I willed the bodies. As if an explosion had suddenly erupted, the passengers shot up and flew through the air. They hit the tunnel walls – brick dust tumbled down. Without thinking, I snatched hold of Jude by the ankles and yanked him free from the tracks. He seemed dazed. In the corner of my eye, I could see Max. He pulled Ben to safety. The sudden whoosh and roar of the train as it passed us had me spinning – tumbling over. I fell against Raven just as she was getting back up on her feet. The suction of the train as it thundered by felt like a magnet, drawing me in. I clung onto Raven. My hair swept wildly about like I was caught up in a hurricane. Bits of bodies rained down as the passengers' limbs were torn from their torsos and sucked under by the speed of the train. A shower of blood sprayed up from the wheels, coating me in a layer of red. I fell to my knees. My body and head suddenly felt overwhelmed with exhaustion. The roar of the train rumbled away down the tunnel as the last carriage passed us. I breathed in deeply.

My heart raced. My head pounded.

The tunnel suddenly filled with the noise of squealing brakes. I looked up. Gone was my vision of red. I stared down into the dark at the train. It was slowing. The metal wheels grated over the rails as the brake was applied. It was some way off in the distance now, but I could still see the train lights.

"Get up."

Ben stood in front of me and offered his hand. I grabbed hold of it. Still feeling exhausted and legs shaky, I let him pull me up.

"We have to leave – now!" he said. "It won't be long before this tunnel is filled with police."

"I'm not sure I can," I whispered, staggering about, my head woozy.

"Now's not the time to be weak," he frowned. "You have to keep going. If you give up now, then all of this has been for nothing. I may as well have given you over to Doctor Middleton instead of giving you the key to your freedom."

"Freedom? This isn't freedom. This is a fucking nightmare..." I gasped.

"You're gonna wish it was just a nightmare if you don't get moving," grimaced Ben. He grabbed hold of my shoulders and manhandled me around. Shoving me forward, he began to frog-march me along the tunnel.

"Stop pushing me!" I snapped, swiping his hand away. "I can fucking walk unaided." I looked over my shoulder. The others followed close behind.

"Speed up," ordered Ben, blocking my view. "Everyone's here, you don't need to stress about them."

"I'm just making sure they're all okay," I scowled. "Unlike you, I have a heart – I care."

"If I didn't care, then I wouldn't be here," said Ben. "All I know is that something very strange happened back there. I was completely overwhelmed by something much stronger than Quint. That's never happened before. Quint was held back – leaving just me to fight whatever that was. It knew that I, alone, couldn't fight back. It wanted to rid Quint of my body."

"It was Doshia," I said, slowing a little so Ben could walk alongside me. "Doshia spoke to me. He said he wanted more. More of what?"

"I don't know much about these Demons other than what Quint lets me know... but I do know that Doshia can't kill Quint. Quint can't kill Doshia, Eras, or the others. They come from the same group... but I think they can kill each other once they have gained full control over the Cleaners. Ridding Quint of the body he has dwelled in for so many years would leave him weak for a while. That's one Demon out of Doshia's way. But what I don't get is why the need for more? I always thought that..." Ben trailed off.

"What?" I pushed.

Shaking his head, he whispered, "I don't know. My head is clouding up. My mind's eye is blocked. Quint doesn't want me to know." Taking hold of my arm gently this time, he picked up pace. "Let's get out of this tunnel. I know we can't see Doshia but that doesn't mean he isn't with us."

Facing front, I sped up. The small pinprick of light in the distance didn't lift the fear that churned away inside me. Daylight was no longer safe.

"Kassidy..." whispered Ben, "I'm ..." He turned his head and stared at me. "I... I'm..." He faced front. "It doesn't matter." He continued to walk forward.

"What?" I touched his arm.

"Nothing," mumbled Ben, shaking his head, "Don't worry."

"Just say it..." I whispered. I could tell he was having trouble in whatever it was that was stuck in his head.

"No, really – it doesn't matter, I've

forgotten what I was going to say. Let's just get out of here." His stare fell back to the ground.

I wanted to push him. I wanted to know what was going on inside his head, but I knew now not to force him. It would only start off a chain reaction with him getting angry, and then me losing it with him, and another argument would break out between us. I decided to let it go. Maybe he would come back at me later.

As I stumbled over the train tracks, I started to think about what had happened in the tunnel. My head felt fogged up. I tried to put everything in order – replay the events that had just taken place. If Doshia wanted to get rid of Ben so Quint would be weak, then that would explain why so many passengers had piled up on top of Ben. Imprisoning him on the tracks would have only led to the ruin of Ben and his body – Quint would have been without a home. Only me, Max, and Raven had had one passenger to contend with – just enough to hold us back so we couldn't help Ben but not enough to have us killed. After all, Doshia needed us – needed our bodies. But what about Jude? Why so many bodies piled up on him? Perhaps Doshia didn't have a use for him. Maybe his body wasn't needed? Jude was the only one from our group who didn't have the black veins. There was no sign of VA20 inside of him. Why keep him? He would be useless to Doshia. I shook my head as a sudden unnerving thought came to mind. Raven's earlier suggestions of not trusting anyone in our group sent goose-bumps over my skin. I took a quick glimpse over my shoulder. Jude was walking a little way behind me. I looked away as our eyes met briefly. I needed to speak to Ben. But would Ben know the answer? Or would I have to wait for Quint to resurface to ask him? I picked up speed. Ben was just a little way in front but I didn't want to speak with him where the others may hear. Determined to catch up with Ben, I pushed forwards.

Someone tapped me on the shoulder. I turned to see Jude trailing behind. My heart sank as I knew I would have to wait for the next opportunity that came to speak with Ben privately.

"Hey, I just wanted to say thanks for helping me back there," said Jude. "If it wasn't for you – I'd be gone – this body of mine would be splattered over the tunnel walls."

"We're in this together, aren't we?" I said, still feeling a little angry with him after what had been said on the train, but feeling a little nervous, also, with suspicious thoughts raging around inside my head.

"Yeah, but you could have got yourself killed. I am grateful," he whispered. "But don't put yourself in harm's way again for me – okay? I'd miss you if anything happened... I know that's probably hard to believe after what I said on the train... but it's true."

"Look – Jude, I'm sorry we had a row and I'm sorry about what happened the other night at the Bishop's. I was messed up that night – tired – confused – scared. I wasn't thinking straight. I didn't mean for that to happen. I really like you, I really do, but... as a friend." I looked down at the ground, feeling awkward.

"I can take that," said Jude, "for now, anyway." He smiled. "When I first saw you at Cruor Pharma, I really liked you. I still do. You actually made me rethink my life. I realised what a shit existence I'd been living. I just want some fun – some friends to hang out with." He stared at me with that cheeky glimmer in his eyes – the same look that had attracted me to him on the first night in the hospital. But was that cheeky glimmer a look to trust? Was I being paranoid again? Only Ben or Quint would be able to put my mind at rest – at least, that's what I hoped.

I could feel my earlier resentment that I'd had for Jude melt away. Who couldn't like him?

Yes, he said the wrong things sometimes – he spoke without thinking, but he had an energy about him, he was dependable – ready to get stuck in. He was good at reassuring me. He made me feel safe. In fact, it had been because of him that I hadn't walked out of Cruor Pharma that night when I'd started to get cold feet. He had reassured me then. Yes, he had been wrong that time and I should have listened to my own gut-feeling, but that wasn't his fault. Or was it?

"You want fun?" I half-smiled, trying to remember the last time I had felt that. "This ain't fun." I stared up at the tunnel roof. "Not sure I'll ever feel that way again." I tried to act casual. If I was wrong in my suspicions then Jude would probably be hurt by my sudden mistrust of him, but if I was right – what would he do if he knew I had discovered the truth about him?

"You will," whispered Jude. "I'll make sure of it."

"Not if those fucked-up Satanist passengers come looking for us!" hissed Raven, leaning in between Jude and me. "The only fun we're gonna have is when we get to Doctor Langstone's – get this shit out of us – and find Max's brother."

"Something tells me it isn't gonna be all that," grimaced Max, catching up with the rest of us. "None of us have any idea what to expect when we get there." He turned and looked at me. "Didn't think we were gonna get all those bodies off of Ben and Jude. Whatever you did, it was pretty amazing."

"I didn't do anything," I said. "The bodies just moved by themselves – I think?" I stared past him back into the dark of the tunnel. Nothing seemed to be following us but did that matter? Doshia seemed to be able to travel amongst us unseen. I wrapped my arms about myself, suddenly feeling a nervous chill race up my spine.

I carried on walking. The light coming from the end of the tunnel had become bigger. I knew we should be running – trying to gain as much distance between us and everything that followed – hunted us. But the energy had gone. My legs felt like two concrete posts. My eyes stung from tiredness, and I just couldn't seem to think straight anymore. One thing I did know, though, was that I wasn't going to be sorry to see the end of this dark, damp tunnel.

I tried to quicken my pace. It was so much effort to keep going. Thoughts of a nice, warm bed, soft pillow, and eyelids that could shut without fear of waking up to find the Cleaners had crept up on me circled around in my mind. I had to stop thinking about it – it was slowing me down. I needed something that would keep my mind sharp – alert. I thought about what Max had just implied a few moments ago. The whole situation in the tunnel had happened so fast. It had been nothing but a nightmarish jumble of crazy people, blood, and the sheer fright alone of nearly being crushed to death by a train was enough to send anyone into meltdown. I had used a knife on someone. Stabbed it through their neck. Did that make me a murderer? It was self-defence – wasn't it? That wouldn't be how the police viewed it. There were a lot of bodies left in the tunnel. It looked more like a massacre. Add the new body count to the one that we had already been framed for – I didn't think self-defence would go down too well in front of a jury. But had it been me that had somehow moved those passengers? I hadn't even been touching them when they suddenly flew off of Ben and Jude. I had willed them to move – that was all. That kind of thing was more suited to Quint. But even Ben had said that Quint had been unable to do anything. Maybe Doshia had done it? No, that didn't make sense. Doshia had wanted them dead. That overwhelming feeling of VA20 had been present when I'd lost it with Raven on the train, when I'd had to fight the man with the knife. But it had been at its strongest out by the track when I thought all was lost in regards to saving Ben and Jude. I looked down at my arms. It was too dark to see clearly and I knew my skin was covered in blood. Could VA20 make me do such things? I stared at the back of Ben, who was still up ahead. *Move – move.* I tried to concentrate – focus on shifting Ben, but nothing happened. I shook my head. *Stupid, I'm so stupid – of course I can't move people.* Perhaps Max had played a part? The two of us combined, both desperate to save Ben and Jude? I really didn't have a clue. I trudged on. My eyes narrowed as daylight filtered through the mouth of the tunnel. The cool air hit my skin as I stepped out. What way now and how were we going to get there?

CHAPTER FOURTEEN

I breathed deeply. The cool autumn air seemed to revive me a little. I looked down at myself. What skin I could see had blood splatters over it. At least I was wearing black clothing – it hid the bloodbath I had just been involved in. I could easily wash my skin and cover up all traces of death that lingered on me. Staring at the others, Max seemed to look the worst. What, with his ripped T-shirt and black veins on show – now he had the added disadvantage of bloodstains over him.

I turned around and took in the view. We still stood on the tracks – a group of lost travellers. Tall trees swayed their branches like brittle bones ready to snap from a strong gust of wind – the curled-up leaves scattered across the rails. I looked back at the mouth of the tunnel and shuddered. My eyes caught sight of a narrow bridge over the tunnel, the road twisting down from over the top of it. Maybe we could follow it? It might lead to somewhere we could clean up. I could hear Jude, Raven, and Ben each putting across their ideas on which way to go. Their voices weren't angry but I could hear the tension in them. Everyone seemed to know where we should be heading. The same argument of whether we should find Doctor Langstone's and not just go on the run cropped up again. I closed my eyes and let out an exasperated sigh. We were just going around and around in circles. Never mind the tension I could hear in them – it was beginning to build up inside of me. Frustration and pure weariness was starting to take hold.

"Shut up!" I screamed. "The plan is to get to Doctor Langstone's – to find Robert – and to get VA20 out of us! How many more times are we gonna waste precious moments talking about it? We should be moving – not bitching at each other." I stood, arms folded across me. Looking at Ben, I glared and said, "I want you to take me to Doctor Langstone. No more of this, *should we–or shouldn't we crap.* I'm going and you're gonna take me." I jabbed my finger in his direction. "If you're really sorry for what you've done to me – then you'll take me – no arguments. And Jude," I turned my attention to him, "as much as I like you, this whole going on the run thing and having fun – it's bullshit! We can't live like that! Look at what's happened to us ever since we left Cruor Pharma. We've had just a small taste of what living on the run is like. And I don't fucking like it!"

"Okay." Jude smiled over at me. "But you

said you liked me – right?" His blue eyes glimmered and his face lit up.

"As a friend," I said, trying to calm myself down. That uncomfortable feeling of VA20 moving around in me made me feel jittery – on edge. That mischievous look in Jude's eyes didn't help. It just brought forward those feelings of suspicion. I had to speak to Ben.

"What way do you want to go then?" asked Ben, walking over so he now stood in front of me. He still looked just as pristine as he did before the massacre in the tunnel. Not a hair out of place – no blood – no creases in his suit – immaculate, like he'd just stepped off of the catwalk from a fashion show.

His smouldering stare had me feeling flustered. His presence leaning over me made me shrink back slightly. Those lips of his were crying out to be kissed. I wanted to reach up and take hold of him. No – I wanted him to take hold of me. I stepped back. I was getting sucked in by him – by Quint. Although there were no signs of him in Ben's eyes yet, I could feel him – sense he was there somewhere deep inside of Ben.

I broke his gaze – his charm. Ben had made it perfectly clear that he felt nothing for me, so I would honour that and not pursue him. As for

Quint, I would need to be strong and not let him lure me into his hypnotizing ways. Regaining my composure, I said, deliberately avoiding Ben's eyes, "Lets follow the tracks. It's the way we were gonna go on the train so it can't be wrong, can it?" It was more a statement than a question. I had every intention of going that way and I glared at the others, waiting for one of them to challenge me over it. No one did.

"Let's go then – lead the way, but stay off the tracks," warned Ben, gesturing me forward to take the lead.

I took hold of his arm and turned my body away from the others. "I need to speak to you." I lowered my voice and stepped in close to Ben.

"What about?" he whispered, lowering his head near to mine so he could hear me.

I risked a quick glimpse at his eyes. Still blue, yet a look of amusement swam in those crystal waters. His lips twitched up into a smile. "Something funny?" I said, trying to sound like I didn't give a shit, but really I did. Was he laughing at me? A quick look at myself to see if there was something wrong – something out of place that had made him smile. Well, apart from the blood stains and black veins, and yes, I probably did look a right mess, there was nothing else that I could see. Was it my face? I reached up and touched my cheeks, running my fingers down to my neck. Had those ugly veins covered more of me? I wished I'd had a mirror. I quickly pulled my hair around my neck and let it hang over the sides of my face. I wanted to cover up. I felt ugly.

"Nothing funny," whispered Ben, still smiling. "It's just you look kinda good when you're angry – a challenge – someone you could have a good time with in bed."

I shot a look at him, "I know that's you, Quint, who's talking. Ben would never say that to me – he's not interested. So instead of hiding in Ben why don't you just come out?" I carried on walking.

"Keep talking angry to me," whispered Quint. "I love it." He reached out and pulled my hair away from my face. "You don't ever need to cover up – you're beautiful."

I slapped his hand away and replaced my hair back where it had been. "I don't feel beautiful," I snapped. "And I'd rather not talk about it. It's just a reminder of how I really look. I don't want you staring at me. I don't want that kind of attention – when you look at me – you see those ugly veins – that's the real reason you were smiling."

"No, it's not," said Quint, taking hold of my arm. "I was smiling at your strength. You're a fighter – I like that about you. And how could I possibly ever think of those black veins as ugly? They're a mark of what's inside you. A part of me now lives in you. You wear the Demon's life under your skin and you wear it well." He took hold of my hand and gently ran his finger over one of the veins. "You're perfect, don't ever think that you're not."

I pulled my hand away and tucked them up inside the sleeves of my top. "You're crazy," I spat. "Do you really think I want to look like this? Do you really think I want one of your Demon Cleaners living inside me? If I'd wanted veins like this, which I don't, then I could have just jacked-up down some side-street in Holly Tree with all the other drug users – it's ugly – and it's ugly inside me – it makes me feel bad!"

"You don't have to have a cleaner inside you," whispered Quint. "I don't want that to happen to you, either. I will keep you safe. We can be together forever. Just you and me, Etta, we can..."

I stopped him mid-sentence. "I'm not Etta, I'm Kassidy," I spat. "Go find this Etta and fuck off! It's because of you and these ugly veins that Ben doesn't like me! Can't you see just how messed up this all is? I've fallen for your charm before, thinking it was Ben – only to be pushed away when Ben manages to overpower you. It's like being on the end of a fucking fishing rod – one minute reeled in – the next cast aside!" I spun around and faced the others, my hands clasped tight against the sides of my face. "Someone, please tell me that I've taken fucking acid and none of this shit is real – please?" I stared at Raven, then Jude, and lastly Max. "Am I on some fucking trip? Did someone spike my drink? Right now, I'd kiss the person who can tell me that's what has happened!" Silence. Just the gentle sound of wind rustling through the trees. I turned back to Quint. "You've fucked my life up good and proper – thank you!" I stormed off along the track completely forgetting that I'd wanted to ask about Jude.

Hands gripped my arms. "I'd like to fuck you up in more ways than one," hissed Quint. "You don't get to walk away from me – ever!"

"Hey, get off her!" shouted Max, shoving Quint hard in the back.

Quint stumbled forward but still held me tight. A struggle of arms waved around. Jude jumped in and joined Max, both trying to release me from Quint.

"Let go of me!" I shouted, twisting and turning from left to right. "I don't want you!"

Quint glared down at me. I could see the anger in his eyes – feel the rage that seemed to swarm about him. It was like a shadowy menace – a dark mass that surged around him. "Without me – you'll be blind. No one will hear you cry out when you sleep – when they come to get you! You're not safe without me." He yanked me forward – the tips of our noses just touching. I could feel his power – a force so strong within him, it scared me. The shadow reared up like black tentacles, swishing and flicking. They whipped about, scattering Jude and Max away like skittles. They yelled out as they hit the ground a few feet away.

"Stop," I breathed. "You're hurting me." I felt crushed from his hold. I struggled to take in air. "Please." I could feel myself weaken. "Let me go."

"Why don't you love me anymore?" Quint softened a little. "I've lost you once before and I don't want to lose you again. We're together now – stay with me, Etta."

"I'm not Etta." I stared up into his eyes. "I don't know who Etta is but it's not me. You've got the wrong person." I cautiously reached up and touched the side of his face. "I'm sorry – you're mistaken." Quint looked at me quietly. He shook his head sadly.

"What did that Demon do to you? All those years ago – what did it do to make you forget who you are?"

It was my turn to shake my head. What did I have to say or do to make him realise that I was Kassidy Bell, not Etta. I pulled away from him slowly, frightened that he might make another grab for me. My eyes caught sight of Raven. She stood behind Quint shaking her head and pulling a dumb face behind his back. Her lips mouthed the word – *crazy*. Ignoring her, I glanced back at Quint, taking another few steps away, out of his reach. I didn't know what to say. So instead I stayed silent, fearing that any denial about me not being Etta might cause Quint to really lose it.

"I'll go anywhere with you – just you and me," whispered Quint. He held out his hand.

"I... I can't," I looked down at the ground, afraid to see his reaction. When nothing was said and the only sound I could hear was the rustling of the trees, I looked up. Quint had retreated, back within Ben. I fell to my knees – relieved that Quint had disappeared for now at least.

"Are you all right?" asked Ben, crouching down beside me. "What happened?"

I stared out across the train tracks. Max and

Jude seemed to be okay after being flung away by Quint. They both walked together, stopping beside Raven. "I'm too exhausted... too confused to explain," I answered Ben. "That Demon in you – Quint, he thinks I'm someone else."

"Who?"

"Etta," I whispered.

Ben fell silent for a few moments. "I don't remember Etta – yet there's something in me that makes me feel like I should know her – something nice – something – I don't know. It's all fucked up in here." He tapped the side of his head.

"So she's real – she really exists?" I asked, clambering back onto my feet.

"I have a strong sense that she's been gone a long time... someone's keeping quiet," he pointed to himself, meaning Quint. "I won't get anything from him unless he decides to let me in."

I glanced over at the others. My eyes fell upon Jude. "Okay, never mind Etta," I whispered, grabbing hold of Ben's arm and pulling him away enough from the others so we couldn't be heard. "I need you to think carefully. I know your head is all mixed up with you and Quint but try to remember." I took a deep breath. "You're a Demon – well, you have one in you. Why would a Demon ever use a placebo? Would Doctor Middleton ever use one... did you ever inject any of the volunteers with a placebo?"

"A placebo?"

"Yes, shhh," I looked back over my shoulder at Jude. "Don't speak so loud. Well... did you... I know proper doctors use them in drug trials but your lot aren't exactly real doctors."

"We were once," glared Ben. "I still am — when I'm myself."

"Just answer the question... please... it's important." I pulled on his arm, a feeling of urgency swept over me. I was praying the answer would be yes. I didn't want to be faced with the realisation that we had been tricked — deceived — lied to by someone who I had trusted. Someone who I had opened up to about my dad.

"There would be no reason for any of the Demons to use something so pointless. They weren't or aren't conducting an experiment for the good of the human race. They don't care about such things. VA20 would have been used on all volunteers. Why are you asking this?"

"Are you sure?" I felt my heart sink only to be replaced with fear. My eyes nervously peered round in Jude's direction. I looked away quickly. Jude was watching us. He stood in between Max and Raven, not listening to them but staring at me and Ben.

"Yes. I'm mixed up about a lot of things, and my memory is hazy, but I know that there were no placebos used."

"You warned me a couple of times not to trust someone in my group but you never told me who or why. Were you talking about Jude?"

"Did I?" Ben narrowed his eyes, "I don't remember."

"Please try," I whispered. "I need to know. Don't you see how important it is? That could be Doshia over there. Inside Jude."

"Hey, what are you two talking about?"

I could feel myself tense at the sound of Jude's voice. I turned around to find him standing just behind me. "Nothing much," I smiled, trying to keep my face natural and not with a look of fear across it.

"Kassidy was just saying that we need to hurry up. The Cleaners will still be following and what, with the police probably on their way..." Ben trailed off.

An awkward silence fell among us. I felt sick, my stomach a jumble of nerves. Had Jude heard what Ben and I had been saying? I chewed on my lower lip. Should I say something? Should I just come out with it and accuse Jude? No, that would be bad. If Doshia was really inside Jude then the game would be up and I had no idea what Doshia would do to me, Max, and Raven. Would he try and kill Ben off once and for all – leaving Quint weak without a body?

"Are you okay?" asked Jude, reaching out and squeezing my arm. "You look really pale. Like you've seen a ghost or had some bad news."

I tried to laugh it off. "Bad news? What could be worse than what we've already been through? I'm fine, I just think we should get going... that's all." I turned my back on him and started to walk alongside the train track.

When I thought there was a safe enough distance between me and Jude – out of earshot – I glanced up at Ben.

"Can you really not remember anything about Jude? Anything about him that maybe Quint let you in on?"

"If there was then Quint is not letting me remember... don't forget, he's one of them. He's not going to give up anything if it means preventing him from doing what it is he's trying to do."

"Why would Quint not tell me? He said he would keep me safe – he wanted me to stay with him. Why not tell me that Jude is Doshia? It makes no sense."

"Kassidy, I've told you before to not trust the Demon in me. Of course none of this makes sense. We know what each Demon is after but we don't know how they're playing it. They manipulate, they get you to trust them, and they make you think you're special and then... they get you to kill for them... and your case... they take your body." Ben peered over his shoulder. "If Jude is Doshia then you need to get away from him... and I need to go..."

"What? Go where?"

"I shouldn't be anywhere near you or your friends. I know I said I would get you in to see Doctor Langstone but... if Quint is asking you to stay with him then that's no good... it's dangerous. He's probably just playing you – doing what Demons do best."

"I don't want you to go... I need your help... I need you, Ben. I know I can trust you – not Quint – you!"

"I told you before – I'm trouble. If I stay well away from you then Quint can't have you." Ben glanced at me. "It's the right thing to do... I know it is... I don't get to do many good things these days but if I can do this, then I will."

"No! You can't just walk away..." I snatched hold of his hand. "There's good in you – in *you*, Ben

– I trust you... I promise I won't ever let Quint fool me... I won't believe him. If I do that, then you can help me and I'll stay safe."

"I don't want to be the one who opens my eyes to see you lying on a floor bleeding out... I don't want to be the one who takes you back to Cruor Pharma, and I don't want to be the one who holds you down while a cleaner enters you and fucks up your head. I can't see that... I've seen too much torment... felt too much pain. You must be fucking crazy to want to stick around me. I'm using *my* head – not Quint's – and I'm gonna leave you."

"What about Jude... you're just gonna leave me here with him – with Doshia?" I could feel myself shaking. My insides seemed to tremble. I didn't want to lose Ben. I looked over my shoulder. Jude walked slowly behind Max and Raven. His eyes stayed peeled to the spot – me. "Don't go... please."

"Enough!" Ben shook my hand free from his. He brushed down his waistcoat and straightened up his jacket like he was preparing to go into an important meeting.

"Quint won't let you leave," I blurted out, a last attempt at getting Ben to stay. "Even if you do leave me now, he'll bring you back... I know he will."

"And I'll do everything I can to stop him," glared Ben. "It's the only way – we have to stay apart."

"At least tell me what to do about Jude?" I whispered.

"You'll know when the time is right." Ben looked down at me. "You don't really think I'm gonna walk away and leave you with Doshia, do you? If it's the last thing I can do to help, then I'll do it. There's a train coming, and if you listen very carefully, you'll hear the sound of sirens." He reached up and stroked the side of my face. "Maybe a long time ago, we could have been together." He dropped his hand away and smiled at me. "Stay safe, Kassidy. Run away when the time is right."

"When what time is right... what are you going to do?"

Ben didn't answer. He stopped walking and waited for the others to catch up.

"What's going on?" asked Jude, his eyes looking at Ben and then me.

"The police are here, look." Ben pointed back towards the bridge that ran over the top of the tunnel. A car had stopped at the centre of it. Its sirens were off but the blue lights flashed brightly.

"Shit, we're in trouble!" shouted Max, panic

in his voice. He spun around, his eyes searching our surroundings. "Where can we hide?"

"There is nowhere to hide," Raven said. "We have to run!"

The sirens suddenly cut through the quiet countryside morning, making me jump. The police had seen us.

"Run where?" yelled Jude, pushing Raven aside. "Which way?"

Another sound cut over the sirens – a train blasting its horn. I looked along the tracks and could see a thunderous lump of metal bearing down the rails. I stood rooted to the spot. A mixture of fear and panic flowed through me, leaving me flustered and unable to make a decision. Which way should we run? And what about Jude? I looked at Ben. He winked and smiled at me. He knew what to do. That look he gave me said everything. This was it. This is where we said a silent goodbye and whatever he had planned for Jude would also be a goodbye to him. I just had to figure out when to make my move without alerting Jude that we were separating.

The train sounded its horn again. The police car made its way over the bridge towards us.

"Get over the other side of the tracks!" yelled Ben, taking hold of Jude and shoving him forward over the rails. "Quickly, before the train comes past and blocks our escape. The police won't be able to follow us while the train comes through." Ben took one last glance at me and ran across the rails – Jude followed, stumbling as he went. Something fell from his pocket and I saw Raven pick it up and place it inside the jacket she wore.

I grabbed hold of Max just as he was about to follow Jude, "No, not with them. Follow me."

"What are you doing?" shouted Max. "We need to get away from the police."

"There's no time to explain," I pulled on his arm, snatching at Raven with my other hand.

"Come on, Kassidy!" yelled Jude. He had reached the other side of the tracks and was now watching – waiting for us to join him. Ben stood silently behind Jude. His blue eyes stared back at me.

Before any of us could reply, the train hurtled by, whipping up the leaves in a shower of reds and yellows, blocking our view of Ben and Jude. The carriages sped by in a blur of metal.

"This way," I pointed up a steep incline dotted with bare, scrawny trees. "Run!"

There was no time for hesitation. We had to get away before the train had moved past and we had to escape from the police. I ran. I didn't even bother to check if Max and Raven were following. If the police caught us, then that would be it. No chance of seeing Doctor Langstone, no way of removing VA20, and no more freedom in more ways than one.

CHAPTER FIFTEEN

As I ran, dodging trees and dips in the ground, I found myself wishing I was a cheetah. I lengthened my stride as far as possible – pushed myself forward. I darted left to right, jumping over lumps of rock, avoiding anything that would be my downfall. The autumn wind rushed through my hair and stung my cheeks. I knew Max and Raven were close behind. I could hear their feet pounding over the ground, their breathing heavy. I focused on what lay ahead. I didn't dare look around.

The hill we were running up seemed endless. If only there was a break in the trees – which looked more like crooked stickmen. The constant darting from left to right slowed me down – messed up my pace. Where were the police? Had they left their car and were now chasing us on foot, or were they traveling along a road – one that I didn't know about or could see? Would they be waiting at the top of this hill for us to come stumbling out of the trees, ready to catch us? Was it Cropper and his men, or was it the local police force who now had an interest in us? So many questions but no time to act on the answers.

"Stop... stop," gasped Max. "I can't see

them, I don't think the police are following us."

"I can't see them either," panted Raven. "I think we've lost them."

I stopped running. Reaching out, I grabbed hold of a branch to steady myself. I heaved in a lungful of air and checked back the way we had run. There certainly were no signs of police chasing us. The hillside seemed void of all life. The wind whistled through the matchstick men trees causing them to shudder and make them look like they were speaking to each other. Above the wind, I could still hear the distant sound of sirens wailing. Maybe the police had gone after Jude and Ben? *Good luck to them,* I thought, they had gone after the wrong group. The police didn't stand a chance facing those two. I shuddered as I thought of Jude. What would he be doing now? How was Ben going to handle him? The very thought of Jude had me on edge. If he really was Doshia then the police would be disposed of pretty quickly but that wouldn't be good. It meant Doshia would soon be back on our heels. It wouldn't take him long to catch up with us.

"We can't stay here," I said. "We're not safe." I turned to start back up the hill.

"Hold on," said Max, flicking his hair from out of his eyes. "What's going on? Why have we left the others?"

"Keep moving and I'll explain," I said, taking a large stride up the hill. "I think Jude is …"

"Eras!" cut in Raven, shoving her hands in her pockets. "I know he is because…"

"No, you're wrong," I snapped, annoyed that she had butted in. "I think he is Doshia."

"What... Doshia..?" Raven looked confused. "Yes… maybe you're right." She took her hands back out from her pockets and scraped a greasy strand of hair behind her ear. "I always knew he couldn't be trusted."

"Are you sure?" questioned Max. "I mean… I thought he was one of us. He's done nothing but help us get away… do you have any evidence to back that up? It's not that I don't trust you, Kassidy, but... Jude?"

"I knew it," hissed Raven. "I said – didn't I… back before we got on that train wreck to hell… how could we trust him. I said when we'd escaped out of Cruor Pharma… it must have been him who had killed Fred Butler." She stood with her hands on her hips. "But no one believed me." She glared with an accusing expression.

Ignoring Raven, Max said, "Tell me why you think this."

I ducked under a low hanging branch as I

continued to climb the hill. "He has no black veins... he said he'd probably had a placebo," I breathed heavily. The climb was beginning to leave me short of breath. "But Demons wouldn't use placebos. Ben said everyone got VA20. So how does that explain no black veins on Jude? Think about it..."

"Oh, I've thought about it ever since clapping eyes on him," said Raven, checking over her shoulder. "I knew there was something dark about him. It explains so much – when we were at Cruor Pharma, I was waiting to have my health check... you know... before they took us to the ward. I started panicking... I wanted to leave. I remember walking out of the waiting area and heading back to the reception. Jude followed me... gave me this nice speech about how he'd done drug trials before and there was nothing to worry about." Raven looked down at the ground as she continued to climb the hill. "He said he'd look after me – reminded me of the money I would get." She shook her head. Her dark, accusing eyes had glistened over. "I believed him – what an idiot I was. I actually trusted him. Now look at me! Look at us!" She wiped a tear away and hung her head low so her face was covered with her hair.

For a brief moment, I felt Raven's pain. I shared it. We all did. It was bad enough to have been caught up in these so-called drug trials but to have been deceived by someone who had been a part of our group – pretended to have suffered like the rest of us – felt like the biggest stab in the back. How could he? How could he just befriend us all, take us on this so-called journey of escape, act like he was one of us? All these questions spun around in my head like a whirlpool – pointless questions as I already knew the answers. He was a Demon and that's what Demons did.

"It all makes sense now," I whispered. "He never wanted to believe in Demons and ghosts. Even when the obvious was staring him in the face. He kept saying it was all nonsense – that such things didn't exist but... he was just trying to cover up the truth. Well, until it became too hard to hide what was going on."

"But he helped us to get away from Alex – from the guy at the petrol station – he got us out the goddamn gates at Cruor Pharma – the very place where I would have thought he would want to keep us. I don't get it," Max said. "He drove us out of Holly Tree in his own car! Are you sure about this?"

"He did all those heroic acts because he wanted us for himself," I spat, feeling angry at myself for being taken on such a ride. "That's why he didn't want Ben tagging along – all of a sudden he had competition – another barrier to get through. He never wanted to go to Doctor Langstone's at first. Why? Because that was another Demon who would get in his way. Then all of a sudden, the mention of the Cleaners needing more bodies probably had him thinking that Doctor Langstone's wasn't a bad idea after all. The hope that your brother, Robert, being there was probably a big draw for him." I turned away from Max and Raven. I didn't want them to see the small puddles beginning to well up in my eyes. Was there anyone out there we could trust? What about Ben? He had covered up the truth to begin with but at least now I knew what he was about. He was either Ben or Quint. But could I really trust either of them?

"Shit," frowned Max. "I can't believe it. I don't want to believe it."

I spun around, blinking away my tears. "It's true! It fits together like a jigsaw. He persuaded Raven and me to stay for the drug trial. He was the last one to see Fred Butler alive. It must have been him who turned off the iPod I was trying to charge at Hannah's flat..." I stopped. *Hannah*. "Oh, god." I brought my hand up to my face, closed my eyes. "Jude killed Hannah. Remember?" I grabbed hold of Max, pulling on his arm. "Max... he killed Hannah! Doshia has the ability to leave his host's body and dwell in others, making them do what he wants them to do. Doshia was there – he spoke to me." I felt sick. Jude had made my best friend jump and kill herself.

"It must have been him in the shower with you," said Raven. "He attacked you."

I nodded my head slowly as more pieces of the jigsaw fell into place. "He never wanted to go to Hannah's... that message in the bottom of the shower tray told me to get out – to leave."

"And it was Jude who asked about your mobile phone and whether you had Hannah's address in a text message," whispered Raven, her eyes roamed nervously about the hillside. "He wanted us out of there, and what better way to do it by putting scary thoughts in our head? He wanted us to believe that the Cleaners would turn up at Hannah's so it would prompt us into leaving."

"Jude killed Hannah," I whispered again, as if I needed to soak it up some more – to believe it.

Max took hold of my hand and gently squeezed it, "If Jude is Doshia then... yes... he killed Hannah. I'm sorry, Kassidy."

"Filthy Demon pig then ate her picnic," spat Raven. "Took her money and splattered her over her car!"

"That's enough, Raven," glared Max. "Kassidy doesn't need reminding." He looked at me, his eyes full of concern. "Are you okay?"

I chewed on my lower lip. It seemed to help stem those tears from materializing into waterfalls. I pulled my hand away from Max. "I'm all right." I wasn't. Not really. But I didn't have time to fall apart. We had probably already wasted precious moments standing on the hillside. "Okay, let's get ourselves together. We're aiming for Doctor Langstone's." I tightened the strap of the satchel around me. "The police are now close behind and we have to keep ahead of Jude. I don't know how Ben is going to handle him – or what Quint will do if he decides to take over Ben, but either way, Doshia is stronger than Quint, so…" I checked down the hillside. The place seemed empty of all life. "So, I don't think it will be too long before Jude is back on our heels."

"Which way do we go? I have no idea how far away we are from Derbyshire. Do you?" asked Max.

I shrugged my shoulders. "The train got us a little nearer but all we can do is keep running along this hill and keep the train tracks in sight. If we follow them, then we can't go wrong."

"Let's stop chatting and get running then," said Raven, brushing past me and Max and breaking into a trot. "Those sirens sound closer to me. We can't get arrested – we'll never make it to Langstone's and we'll never find your brother." She glanced over her shoulder at Max before heading along the side of the hill.

We followed close behind, making sure to keep the tracks within sight. Pushing through the matchstick men branches that seemed to want to snare us in their brittle arms, I couldn't help but think we weren't going to make it. There was so much to lose. The police would never believe our story. We couldn't fall now. We had to keep going. We had to keep running.

CHAPTER SIXTEEN

It felt like we had been running forever. Where did I get my energy from? Fear. The thought of being chased – hunted, kept my legs moving. I had to stop myself from turning around – from peering over my shoulder to see if we were being followed. I didn't want to know.

Every now and then I could see the train track. It seemed to circle around the bottom of the hill. Would we have to break cover soon and run across open land? I pushed on, my feet pounded the crisp leaves scattered over the hillside. I could still hear the sirens. They hadn't got any nearer but hadn't faded, either. We weren't making any headway. Would we ever outrun the police? Raven stopped abruptly.

"We need to head up and over this hill," she gasped breathing in the cold air. "The track is running to the right. There's no point in going round – we have to go over." She pointed up through the trees, bending at the waist to catch her breath.

"Okay," I puffed. "Don't stop... keep going... we haven't got time."

"Don't know how much longer I can keep running," gasped Max, as we changed direction and took on the steep hill.

"You have to," I said, clambering over a toppled tree trunk. "We can do this... when we get to the top it will be all downhill after."

Max pushed himself on. It was clear to see that we were slowing, though. After all, we had been on the run since the early hours of the morning and prior to that – clambering up and down chimneys during the night.

As we cleared through a large cluster of trees, we suddenly found ourselves standing beside a road covered on both sides with more bony trees. I looked to my left. The road was clear. I turned to my right and gasped. A police car was parked alongside the twisting road, tucked slightly under the canopy of the withered trees. We stood still – silent for what seemed like forever until the driver's door swung open and out stepped a policeman.

"Stop!" he yelled.

"Go... go!" I pushed Max forward.

"Head for the other side..." shouted Raven, already halfway across the road.

"Stop, Police!" the officer shouted again. I glanced over at him as I ran across the road. It wasn't Inspector Cropper. It must be one of the local police officers. I carried on running, aware that another police car had just pulled around the bend in the road and was now heading towards us. The air was suddenly filled with the piercing wail of sirens and the trees lit up in flashes of blue. I reached the other side of the road and burst through the hanging branches that blocked my way. I could hear more vehicles, the wheels squealing as brakes were applied. My heart pounded. It seemed that the entire police force was on the hill.

"This way," screeched Raven, snatching hold of my wrist and pulling me further into the woods.

I stumbled and tripped. My face was under attack from the branches springing back from where Raven pushed through in front of me. Max staggered alongside us. His hair snagged on twisted twigs. His face was a mask of fear and determination. My feet slipped on the wet mush of leaves as we descended down the hill. The trees were thicker on this side. It was dark and I couldn't see the bottom of the hill. My heart sounded like it was inside my head – *boom-boom-boom*. There was movement behind us. Footsteps thudding. Voices shouted.

"Police – stop!"

I swayed through the trees – disorientated.

Raven breast-stroked her way through at speed —
the branches fought back. The further down we
went, the thicker the trees got.

"Come on," I yelled at Max, as he had fallen
a little way behind. I stretched out my arm and he
grabbed hold of me. I wasn't going to leave him
behind. We stayed together — even if that meant
we got caught.

"If they get us…" gasped Max, "you need to
hide that passport…"

I looked down at the satchel as I continued
to lurch through the trees. I unfastened one buckle
and slipped my hand into the satchel. My fingers
snatched about until I had Sylvia Green's passport
clutched in my hand. I nearly toppled over as I tried
to push the passport down inside my boot.
Satisfied that it wouldn't fall out, I continued to
elbow my way through, trying to follow in Raven's
path.

"Stop, police!" Several voices filled the air.
"Stop, or I'll release the dogs!"

"Shit, they've got dogs." I looked at Max.
"We can't outrun them!"

"We have to try, come on!" Max yelled,
taking the lead and pulling me along behind him.

The sounds of barking and snarling seemed
to overpower the wail of the sirens. The dogs'

howls were enough to have me barging my way through the trees and clambering over fallen branches like a bulldozer. I could see Raven just up ahead of us, she was ploughing her way across the undergrowth, her arms and head poking out like she was wading through a strong current of water. I kept Raven in sight, following in her path. Did she even know where she was heading? Did she know how to get off this hillside? I sure as hell didn't. I was completely lost – overwhelmed by the shouts of the officers, the sirens, and the barking. The undergrowth and trees were like a maze of snatching hands – pulling and tearing.

Raven suddenly turned around and yelled, "This way! It's clearer through here."

She turned back and continued to run. Just as Max and I reached the clearing, a huge dog leapt out from the cover of the trees and toppled Raven to the ground. She fell flat on her face. The dog snarled and growled, pinning her to the leafy-covered floor of the wood. I could hear Raven scream. In my panic to avoid the dog, I darted to the left. Max went right. We scattered. Separated. Parted ways. But we didn't get very far. As I ran as fast as I could, jaws suddenly clamped down on my sleeve. I fell forward, hitting the ground with a thud. The barking and growling was deafening. I tried to pull my arm away. The dog held on, shaking its head and pulling me across the clearing. My free hand tried to source out something I could hang onto. Something that would give me a bit of leverage to pull myself up onto my knees. But it was no use. The dog was too strong. Its jaws held me down in its vice-like hold. The more I struggled, the tighter its teeth held on.

"It's got me, I can't get it off!" Max shouted.

I couldn't see him but he didn't sound too far from where I lay.

"Don't tell them anything!" screamed Raven. "They won't believe us anyway."

I stayed still. There was no point in struggling against this dog – not unless I wanted my hand ripped off. I waited. Any minute now, I would be arrested. My mind was no longer on escape. Instead, it ticked overtime in how I was going to blag my way out of a cell.

CHAPTER SEVENTEEN

I could hear heavy footsteps approaching. I tried to look up. The dog tightened its jaws around my sleeve and continued to snarl.

"Lay still!" a male voice sounded just above my head.

I tried again to see who was there.

"Lay still – lay still – don't look up!"

I waited. Another set of footsteps approached beside me.

"Off!"

The dog released me. I tried to move but both arms were taken hold of and brought round my back. I could feel the cold metal of handcuffs as they were fastened around my wrists.

"I'm arresting you on suspicion of murder. You do not have to say anything but it may harm your defence if you do not mention, when questioned, something you later rely on in court," someone said.

I was stood up. I looked down to make sure that I still had Father Williams' satchel. It was still there. My eyes met the stare of the officer who had arrested me. He was in uniform. His face looked stern but his brown eyes seemed warm. I looked away, fearful he could see the truth right through me. Murder. I was being arrested for murder. I felt shaky, sick. My head spun. Which murder was I wanted for? How much did the police know? Had I been framed for what had happened at Cruor Pharma? Had Doctor Middleton been unable to cover up what he had done on Ward 2 and had now blamed us? Was it for the murder of Nurse Jones? Fred Butler? Father Williams? Hannah? The Bishop and Alex? The police? Or was it for all those passengers on the train? The list was endless. I took a deep breath. I couldn't shake off that sickening feeling of fright that was eating away inside me. I hadn't murdered those people. But it sure as hell probably looked that way. I was innocent. I tried to go over all the deaths in my head. Innocent, innocent. I ticked off everyone who had been killed with a mental note that I hadn't been responsible. I couldn't possibly be charged for murder. I chewed on my lower lip, my heart suddenly weighed down. I had stabbed that passenger in the neck. It was self-defence!

I was shaken from my thoughts by the sound of more footsteps approaching. I looked to my left and saw Raven and Max. They too had been handcuffed and were now being led back up the hillside. They looked at me with a weary gaze as they stumbled back through the undergrowth.

"Dave," the officer who was walking Max up the hill called out.

"What?"

"You might want to take a look at this one," said the officer, nodding his head at Max. "Drugs."

"I'll take a look when I get this one back to the van," said Dave, leading me through the trees.

I clambered my way back to the top of the hill, the copper named Dave keeping hold of my arm. I stayed silent. Some of the police cars had already left, leaving just a small vehicle and one big van. I guessed that was where Max, and Raven, and I would be put. The back doors were swung open. The officer holding Max walked him over to Dave.

"Take a look."

They were silent for a few moments before Dave stepped in front of Max, a frown across his face.

"What drugs have you been taking?"

"I don't take drugs," answered Max, keeping his eyes lowered.

"Your arms are covered with thick, black veins and you want me to believe that you don't take drugs?" questioned Dave. He turned his attention to me. "What about you? Your veins are the same. I noticed it when I put the handcuffs on you."

I shrugged my shoulders. What could I say?

"This freak has them, too," the other officer said, checking Raven's cuffed wrists.

"Well?" pushed Dave, his eyes wandered from Raven, to me, then fell on Max.

Max shook his head.

"Okay," sighed Dave, "lets load them in the van. We can talk about this back at the station."

The silence on top of the hill was suddenly filled with the static hiss coming from Dave's radio. He turned away from us.

"Bravo-Golf-41 to control," said Dave.

The voice coming from the radio spoke, "Go ahead."

"Got three people under arrest for suspicion of murder," stated Dave, turning back to look at us.

"We'll notify custody," came the response.

"Obliged for that," answered Dave, leaning into his radio which was attached just below his shoulder. "ETA – 20 minutes."

The voice spoke again from the radio, "Custody is full. You will have to take them to Carden Police Station."

"Carden?" moaned the officer who had arrested Max. "That's miles away."

"Bravo-Golf-41 – will head to Carden – over." Dave shook his head as if the thought of going to Carden was the worst news ever.

"Bloody Carden – that's not too far from Millar's Dale Bridge. It's gonna take at least 40 minutes to get there," groaned the other officer.

"Can't be helped, Eric," said Dave, taking hold of Raven and herding her towards the back of the van.

"Carden – Millar's Dale Bridge?" The words had slipped out of my mouth before I realised I'd said them out loud.

"So you do speak then," said Dave, turning to look at me.

I ignored his comment and looked at Max, then Raven. Max stared back, a puzzled look in his eyes but Raven knew what I was thinking. A shine to her eyes told me she remembered.

"Sylvia," I whispered.

"Who?" said Dave. He had now stopped pushing Raven towards the van and stood with his hands on his hips. "What did you say?"

"Nothing." I shook my head and took a sideways glance at Max. He winked at me. He remembered, too.

"Let's just get them in the van," ordered Dave. "It'll be way past lunch before we get to

Carden and..."

"Fog!" I yelled, nearly falling over.

Max and Raven turned around.

"Fucking hell, they don't stop, do they?" said Max. He looked at the two police officers.

"What's the problem?" asked Dave. "It's just a bit of fog."

"It's what's in the fog that's the problem," spat Raven, glaring at Dave.

Eric, with a smile across his face said, "I know what's in the fog." He looked at Dave. "Fog!" He took hold of Max and pushed him up into the van. "Off their heads – bloody junkies."

Dave turned back to Raven to load her in but she had already climbed in. "Wish all our arrests were that keen to come to the station." He looked at me, amused as I pushed past him, desperate to get in.

"Slow down – slow down or you're gonna bump your head," said Dave taking hold of my arm. "What's the sudden rush? It's just some fog."

"No, it isn't," I whispered, staring over his shoulder. The fog was shifting. It weaved its way through the trees like tendrils of floating snakes. It was still slow yet moved a little quicker than I had ever seen it. The Cleaners were in there – somewhere – shrouded amongst the haze. They wouldn't want us arrested. Not by a police force that wasn't part of Inspector Cropper's team. "Please, can we just go?" I looked up into Dave's eyes. "I know this will sound crazy to you... but..."

"Don't say anything!" Raven suddenly screeched from the back of the van.

"Ignore her," ordered Dave. "You were saying?"

I looked down, that anxious feeling biting away at me. If I told him about the fog, would that go against me? Would I be classed as crazy like Sylvia Green and end up locked away in an asylum? But if I didn't say anything, the Cleaners would get us and these two police officers would end up on the ever-increasing murder list that we were wanted for. I looked back at the fog. It had reached the road.

"The fog will kill you!" I blurted out. "Please, we have to get away from here... it will get you, too!"

"That's what taking that shit does to you," piped in Eric, looking at me. "Some kind of acid I reckon, Dave."

"No, it's not!" I shouted. "We are gonna die and so will you if you don't get moving!" I struggled against my handcuffs.

"She's bloody tripping, let's just get her in

the van and get going, Dave." Eric shut one door over and waited for Dave to respond.

"Please... hurry!" I begged.

I looked up at Dave. Did he believe me? His warm eyes looked concerned. Was that just because he believed I was high on drugs, or did he think I was telling the truth? He glanced down the road at the fog.

Not wanting to stand on the road waiting for the fog to reach us, I climbed into the van. Two benches ran down both sides of the vehicle.

I breathed a sigh of relief as the door was shut, leaving the van in semi-darkness. I sat opposite Raven and Max. Peering out through the small window, I could see the fog lingering across the road. I couldn't see the trees anymore. They were swallowed up in the dense mist.

"Come on, come on," I whispered, willing the two police officers to hurry up and get us off the hill.

"How near is the fog?" asked Raven, trying to lean forward so she could see out the window.

"If we don't get moving, we're in trouble," I whispered.

"Hurry up!" screamed Raven, stamping her feet up and down. "The fog's coming!"

A hatch slid open, and from the driver's cab,

Dave's face appeared. He looked annoyed.

"Be quiet," he ordered. "And sit back." He shut the hatch over.

I stared back through the window. The fog had floated further towards the police van. "It's gonna reach us," I said, yanking on my handcuffs. If only I could get them off. If only I could run away. We had eluded the fog on foot so far, but now, handcuffed and locked away in a static van, we didn't stand a chance.

The engine suddenly started and I felt the van rumble into life. It slowly pulled away.

"Thank God for that!" said Max, leaning his head back against the side of the van. "I thought that was it. I thought it was over for us."

"Don't get too relaxed," hissed Raven. "We're not out of trouble yet." She wriggled about on the bench trying to find a comfortable way to sit handcuffed. "Although... we have got a ride nearer to where we were heading."

"Not much use handcuffed and probably heading for a cell," mumbled Max, peering out through the back window. "It won't take the Cleaners too long to find us locked behind bars."

I sat back, satisfied for now that we had gained some distance from the Cleaners. But Max was right. It was only a matter of time before the

Cleaners drifted into Carden Police Station. Then what? I couldn't see us persuading the police not to put us behind bars.

"How are we gonna play this?" I whispered, not wanting the officers to overhear me.

"I don't know," shrugged Max. "What can we tell them? We don't even know what murder we've been arrested for."

"The ones on the train track, of course," said Raven, sliding to the left as the van turned sharply on the road. "It has to be. We know the Cleaners have been tidying away what we've left behind. That's how they work — it's how Middleton wants it to be. But for the first time, the Cleaners didn't keep up with us. The train put too much distance between us and them and they couldn't reach that carnage in time before the police were alerted to what had happened." She slumped back against the side of the van. "Middleton must be pulling his hair out!" Raven smiled underneath her greasy hair.

"That's nothing to smile about," I whispered. "That just makes him more determined to get us back before we spill on him and what he does at Cruor Pharma."

Raven sat quiet for a few moments. She suddenly leant forward and whispered, "We should act crazy – insane. When they get us out of this van, we should act nuts!"

"Why?" frowned Max.

"Because we're being taken to Carden," she grinned.

"So? How will that help us, except a ride to the asylum," I glared. "I don't intend on another hospital adventure from hell, thanks, Raven."

"That's how Sylvia Green escaped the clutches of Cruor Pharma," hushed Raven, checking that the hatch was still closed. "Middleton wasn't interested in her when she got sanctioned for being insane. She's been locked up in there for three months now and he hasn't bothered with her."

"That's because the VA10 didn't work on her," I said. "She was no use to him. Sylvia's mad rants about Cruor Pharma fell on deaf ears. As far as everyone was concerned, she was insane, and therefore, Middleton had nothing to worry about – no one came snooping around him and his hospital. It was the perfect cover for him." I looked at Max. "But we're different. We haven't gone crazy like Carly, Wendy, or Alex. We're the perfect hosts for Middleton's Cleaners and he knows it. He will come for us – and so will Doshia."

"Kassidy's right," whispered Max. "They

won't leave us alone until they have us back at Cruor Pharma."

"But Sylvia might know something that could help us," pushed Raven. "She was the last one to see your brother. She would know if he had been all right. If he had stayed sane."

Max fell quiet. He stared down at his feet.

"She'll know if he was heading for Langstone's for sure," whispered Raven, peering around at the hatch.

"We have no idea of her mental state," I said, nearly falling off the bench as the van hit a bump in the road. "She could be dangerous – like Alex. And besides, even if we did get sent to Carden Asylum, how would we ever find her? We don't even know how big the place is. Sylvia's probably locked up – unreachable."

"Well, what else do you suggest?" said Raven as she glared at me with her dark eyes. "They'll probably send us there anyway. Look at the state of us! Veins full of Demon venom, dried blood all down us, and fucking talons that could be classed as an offensive weapon!" She tapped her nails on the side of the van behind her as if to prove her point.

"We'll probably be held for questioning at the station for 48 hours," whispered Max.

"Long enough for the Cleaners to reach us!" spat Raven. "Whatever we do, we can't be locked away at the station. I'd rather take my chances at the asylum."

"What happens after the 48 hours are up?" I asked.

"Either they charge us, let us go, or grant us bail, I think," whispered Max, peering back out of the window.

"We'd never get bail," I said, "not for murder."

"Why not?" Raven leant forward, "They give bail to all sorts of scum!"

I shook my head. We wouldn't be lucky enough for that. And besides, the 48 hours of questioning would keep us trapped long enough for the Cleaners to catch up. What could we do? I didn't like Raven's idea of being sent to the asylum. It seemed pointless. It would just be another place to get locked up in and I felt pretty sure that the Cleaners would have no problems in getting to us. Just because they'd left Sylvia Green alone didn't mean the same would happen to us.

"Listen," whispered Raven. "We don't want to get questioned by the police and the only way of avoiding that is to act crazy. We won't be fit for questioning, which means the police will have to have us checked over by some doctor." She peered round at Max. "The doctor will tell the police we are unfit and need to go to a hospital." She stopped and took a deep breath, her eyes falling on me. "We get inside the asylum, find Sylvia, take her with us, and break out – job done!" She leant back against the van, a smile on her face like she'd just delivered the greatest speech ever.

"It's too risky," whispered Max. "It all sounds so easy but there's no guarantee that everything you've just suggested will fall into place. They might not send us to Carden – we might end up being sent to the local hospital instead. They might not even send us anywhere! The police might not believe our pretence at insanity." Max closed his eyes and shook his head, then after a short silence, he looked up and stared at me. "I think we should just tell them the truth... tell them everything that's happened. What have we got to lose?"

We fell silent. Only the rumble of the van could be heard. After 10 minutes or so of silence, Raven, who had sat with her head hung low, suddenly sprang forward, almost falling from off the bench.

"Okay!" she said. "Lets tell them the truth – everything! See how quick we all end up inside the asylum. I don't care, that's where I want to go, so I'm up for it! They won't ever believe such a story. They'll think we're all loony!"

I looked at Max. "As much as I hate to say it... I think Raven's right. However we play this... it's gonna end with all three of us in the nut-house. The truth isn't always believed. I'd find it a hard story to believe if someone told me it – wouldn't you?"

Before Max could answer, Raven sat forward and whispered, "So we're all agreed then? We just tell them the truth and wait for our ride into the asylum."

"I guess," murmured Max. He looked defeated... ready to give up.

I shifted along the bench so I was sitting right in front of him. I wished I could give him a reassuring hug. I knew what he was thinking. Would he ever get to Langstone's and find his brother.

"Max," I spoke softly. "Don't give up. We'll find a way out of this... we will find your brother." The words came out easy but deep inside, I wasn't sure if I believed them myself.

CHAPTER EIGHTEEN

For the rest of the journey to Carden Police Station, we stayed quiet. Lost in our own worries and fears. I wondered about Ben. Was he even alive? Had Jude killed Ben when he'd realised that his real identity had been discovered? What about Quint? He would survive, but without Ben's body he would be weakened, at least until he'd found a new host to live in. I stared out through the wire mesh that covered the back window of the van. I didn't want to think about Ben dying so I focused my attention on the outside world. I saw that we had entered a small town. My heart began to race. I looked at Max and Raven.

"I think this is it," I whispered. "I think this is Carden."

The van turned right and slowed. Large iron gates closed behind us as we entered the back of the police station. The van came to a halt as it stopped in a marked parking bay.

"Remember," muttered Raven, "just tell the truth."

The doors to the van opened. Dave and Eric ushered us out.

"Let's get these crackheads booked in and

then I'm off to get some grub," said Eric, checking the time on his watch. "Hope the canteen's still open; it's gone past 3 o clock."

Dave took me by the arm and walked me in through a back door, down some grubby-looking corridor and into a large room with a counter. Behind it stood an older guy, probably in his late forties. Another officer was stacking paperwork neatly into a pile. I looked over my shoulder. Max and Raven stood just behind me. Eric, who wanted his lunch, tapped his foot impatiently. He herded Max and Raven forward as if this would hurry up the procedure of getting us booked in.

"Hello, Dave," said the policeman behind the counter. "Haven't seen you over here for a while. All full up down your end, is it? Been nicking too many people, have you?" He smiled at Dave.

"Alright, Sarge," nodded Dave. "Yeah, custody's full at Draper Station."

"What 'ave we got here then?" asked the Sergeant, looking at me. His grey eyes narrowed as he stared at the three of us.

"They've been arrested on suspicion of murder," said Dave, bringing me forward so I was standing right in front of the Sergeant at his desk.

"What are the grounds for arrest?" he asked Dave.

"They were spotted running from a suspected murder scene at Garner Tunnel. When asked to stop, they ran. They were given every opportunity to stop but didn't. Had to get the police dogs out to stop them."

"I see," mumbled the Sergeant, turning to look at us. "I'm authorising your detention at this police station so enquiries can be made into the offence for which you have been arrested." He looked at Dave, "Remove their handcuffs, please."

I felt the cold metal of the cuffs drop away. Bringing my arms around, I twisted my wrists, relieved to have them free again.

"Hold out your arms for me, please," ordered the Sergeant as he began to inspect my wrists. "Any injuries?"

I shook my head waiting for his response to the black veins snaking around my wrists. He flinched and blinked his eyes several times as if he had seen wrong.

His stare had become cold, wary. "You take drugs?"

"No, I don't," I said, taking a deep breath. "This was injected into me."

"Sarge," said Dave, "the other two are the same." He took hold of Max and pulled him forward. "See."

"Wait there for a minute," ordered the Sergeant. He turned his back to us and started typing away on the computer. A moment later he was back, a puzzled look across his face.

"You say you were injected with something?" he asked, scratching his head.

Before I could answer, Dave piped in, "Sarge, I'm sure it's drugs – some kind of hallucinogen. They were claiming that the fog had something in it, which was going to kill them and us."

"It's true!" spat Raven, shoving past me and Max so she could stand in front of the Sergeant. "And if you keep us here, the fog will catch up and kill us – even *you*."

Eric stepped forward and pulled Raven back. "Whatever they've been taking, it's really messed up their heads."

The Sergeant leant over the counter and said, "Where do you three come from?"

"Holly Tree," I answered.

"Bit out of your way, isn't it? What's brought you this far north?"

"We need to see a Doctor called Langstone. He works at Cruor Pharma's sister company somewhere near here," butted in Raven. "If we don't see him soon then this stuff in our veins is gonna kill us."

"How is this doctor connected to you?" asked Dave. "Why him?"

"Because this shit was injected into us at Cruor Pharma on Strangers Hill... Doctor Langstone used to work there and he knows what this shit in our veins is," Raven glared.

"What is it that's been injected into you?" Dave asked.

"We're not too sure," said Max, glancing at Raven and me, "but we think it's..."

"It's Demon crap!" blurted out Raven. "Demons are after us... they want our bodies so the Cleaners can live in them. The doctors at Cruor Pharma are all Demons. They've killed loads of people and..."

"Enough!" ordered the Sergeant. He turned to look at Dave. "I'm not happy to question them until they've been checked over by a doctor and had a psychiatric assessment."

Raven turned and winked at me.

"Grace, will you remove her jacket?" said the Sergeant, frowning at Dave. He looked troubled. A young police woman who had just strolled into custody came forward.

"I'm not taking off my jacket," snapped Raven, wrapping her arms tight around her.

"Yes, you are," said Dave, prising her arms open while Grace unzipped the leather jacket.

Raven tutted as the jacket was removed. She hugged her arms tight about her, glaring at the flowery blouse she wore.

Dave held out his hand. "Give me the bag."

I glanced down at the satchel. Reluctantly, I handed it over. I watched as Dave emptied out the contents across the counter, the Sergeant picking up each item and checking it over.

He flicked through the pages of Father Williams' diary – not bothering to read any of it. Next he picked up the Bible and opened it to a page which had been bookmarked with a prayer card.

He stared at me. "Resist the devil, and he will flee from you," mumbled the Sergeant, closing the Bible and placing it back into the satchel. "Did you highlight that quote?"

"No, the Bible belonged to Father Williams, as does the diary," I answered.

He looked at Dave, who had just finished watching Raven and Max empty out their trouser pockets. "We'll hold them in the cells and wait for them to get assessed by the FME. There's similarities to another case I've been dealing with here. I trust CID is dealing with this case?"

"They've been informed, Sarge. Probably down on the tracks where the offense took place," answered Dave.

I looked at Max. He stared back. What was the other case that the Sergeant had mentioned? Was it to do with Robert, Max's brother?

"Your names, please," asked the Sergeant, fingers poised over the keyboard.

"We're not giving you our names," hissed Raven. She glared at me and Max. "Don't tell them our names!"

Ignoring her, the Sergeant checked through our items again, looking for any form of identification.

"It will make this whole process easier and quicker if you just give us your names," said Dave. He held his open hand out in front of me. "I need to take that chain you have around your neck, please."

I shot my hand up and took hold of the rosary beads. I didn't want to part with these. They were my protection. Not much, I knew, but, they were something. "Why?" I asked, rolling the beads between my hands.

"You can't take them into the cell with you, that's why," said Dave. "Don't worry, you'll get them back."

I pulled the chain over my head and dropped it into his hand.

"There's nothing here with any identification," grumbled the Sergeant, turning the iPod over in his hands.

I watched as he tried to turn it on. Nothing happened. He tucked it back into the satchel. "Okay, we'll just have to manage for now without their names. After they've been checked by the Doctor we'll take fingerprints and identify them that way," said the Sergeant. He turned to look at Grace. "Cells 5 and 6 can be used. Mark it up on the board." He nodded at a whiteboard attached to the wall.

"I'll run some checks," said Dave. "We know they've come from Holly Tree. I'll check with the locals. Maybe they'll know who we are dealing with."

"No!" I grabbed hold of his arm. "No, you can't do that!"

"Seems to me you have something to hide," said Dave, removing my hand from off his arm.

"Don't do it," said Max. "Please. They'll take us away – back to Cruor Pharma."

"Who's they?" questioned the Sergeant, leaning over the counter.

"Inspector Cropper," I shuddered. The very

name brought goose bumps over my flesh. "If he finds out we're here then he'll come and get us."

"Been up to no good in Holly Tree, have you?" The Sergeant looked at Dave. "Get on it. Contact this Cropper and see what he has to say."

"No!" hissed Raven. "He works for Middleton... he covers up all that Demon shit in Cruor Pharma!"

"That's a very strong allegation you're making against an officer – an Inspector, at that," glared the Sergeant.

"Please... you have no idea what that man is capable of," I blurted out. "Doctor Middleton pays him to keep quiet. He's bent and so is the rest of the force who works alongside him."

"I've heard enough!" said the Sergeant. "Take their shoes and get them in the cells."

Dave and Eric came forward.

"Shoes," ordered Dave. He watched Raven as she flung her shoes with the bows across the room.

"Here!" she snapped. "You're welcome to them."

I unzipped one boot and pulled it off. How was I going to hide Sylvia Green's passport from them now? Did it matter? The reason I had taken it from Ward 1 was to prove that what had happened inside Cruor Pharma was true. Why hide it now? Surely it could only help us.

"I have this," I confessed, pulling out the passport and handing it to Dave.

"At last," he smiled, "we have some ID." He flipped it open to the page with the photograph. His eyes narrowed as he checked the picture and then checked me. "This isn't you." He looked back at the page, his eyes scrolled down. I watched him mutter the name under his breath – "Sylvia Green."

"What did you say?" asked the Sergeant, flipping open a hatch in the counter and coming around to where I stood with Dave.

"This passport belongs to "Sylvia Green," said Dave, handing it over to the Sergeant. "Does this mean something to you?"

"It does," answered the Sergeant. "Where did you get this from?"

"Ward 1 at Cruor Pharma," I said, remembering how we had come across it tucked inside a large clear plastic bag full of brown envelopes. "If you shake the passport a form should fall out. It's a consent form signed by Sylvia agreeing to participate in a drug trial at the hospital." I looked at Max and Raven. I wasn't sure if they were annoyed that I had given up the passport so easily but we had agreed to tell the police the truth.

"You may as well see this one then," said Max. He rummaged around the inside of his jeans and pulled out Robert's passport. "Here." He gave it to Dave.

"Robert O'Brien," said Dave. "Did you get this one from the same place?"

"Yes," whispered Max. "It belongs to my brother. He did a drug test at Cruor Pharma the same time as Sylvia Green. He's been missing ever since."

"Drug tests," exclaimed the Sergeant. "Seems more like drug use! So far, all I've heard is nonsense about Demons, bent coppers, and stolen passports." He looked back over his shoulder at Father Williams' satchel, Bible, and rosary beads. "I believe that you three are part of some strange cult, fuelled on with the use of drugs."

"What?" shrieked Raven. "You're not listening! It's true, all of it! There are Demons out there! They want us back. They want our bodies for the Cleaners!" She flung her arms out, gritted her teeth, and lunged forward. "When are you gonna get it into your thick heads that we are in danger?"

"Calm down," shouted Grace. She took hold of Raven and pulled her back.

"I've heard this all before," said the

Sergeant, shaking his head. He turned to Dave. "I had a young lady in here not too long ago – Sylvia Green. She was deemed insane and locked up in Carden Asylum. She told a similar story but it was obvious it was all down to drug misuse. She's been under some program for the last few months and she's been cleared well enough to be interviewed. I don't know what crap you've been injecting into yourselves in Holly Tree, but whatever it is, it's landed you all a trip to the asylum."

He looked at the other officer, the one called Eric. "I'd like you to ring the asylum. Tell them what we have here." Then, staring at Dave, he added, "Take them to the cells..."

The door to the custody suite suddenly flew open. Two officers barged in, and shuffling in between them was Sylvia Green.

CHAPTER NINETEEN

Sylvia Green was handcuffed and wore a hospital gown underneath a thick, white coat. Her blonde hair was messed up – knotted and matted like it hadn't seen a comb for some time. Her heavy eyelids drooped over her blue eyes, and her mouth hung open a little, revealing several teeth that looked more like black stumps. I felt myself shrink back. Sylvia no longer looked like the nineteen-year-old in her passport photo. She moved across the custody suite like a ninety-year-old. My stomach knotted. I suddenly felt afraid. Her very presence had me on edge. Her face was covered in thick, black veins that bulged so much it made her skin stretch tight. The whites of her eyes had clusters of pooled blood. How had she been deemed fit enough for questioning? Why had she been brought from the asylum to the police station? I took a step back as the two officers holding onto her brought her towards the Sergeant.

"Are you sure about this?" I questioned, my eyes never leaving Sylvia. "Is she safe?"

"Of course she's safe," answered the Sergeant. He looked at Grace, who was still standing beside the whiteboard. "Mark her down for cell 7."

"What!" Max screwed up his nose. "You're putting her in a cell next to us? Are you out of your mind?" He looked at Dave as if he was hoping for some kind of help.

"Sarge... are you sure she's fit to be interviewed? She really doesn't look well," questioned Dave, eyes wide as he stared at Sylvia.

"She looks messed up," shouted Raven. "She looks fucking insane!"

Paying no attention to Raven, the Sergeant glared at Dave. "Wind your neck in, sunshine, and remember who you're talking to. I'm in charge of this custody suite and it will pay you to remember that." He turned to the two officers who had brought Sylvia in. "Remove her handcuffs."

"No!" I shouted. Images of Howard, Carly, and Alex flooded my head. "You don't understand... she's dangerous... she'll kill us all!" I pulled on Dave's arm. "I've seen people like this before... they act like zombies... they can crawl up walls and across ceilings... she'll rip our flesh off with her teeth..."

"Calm down, love," said Eric. He stepped forward and took hold of my arm. "That's just the drugs messing with your head. A little trip to the asylum will sort you out."

"Didn't sort her out though, did it?!" screeched Raven, coming to stand behind me. "What kind of fucking treatment leaves you like that?"

"Don't take drugs then," Eric sneered. "You've only got yourselves to blame."

"We didn't take drugs and neither did she!" shouted Max. "It was injected into us by doctors who assured us it was a simple drug test."

I held my breath as I watched the handcuffs come away from Sylvia's wrists. The room fell silent. Even the police officers seemed suddenly unsure. Was it because they could see the sheer terror in our eyes? Had our pleas to not un-cuff her finally sunk in? Or was it because Sylvia slowly turned her head and grinned? She peered out from her matted hair. The black stumps in her mouth seemed to get bigger as her lips stretched into a wide snarl.

We all took a step back. It was like unleashing a wild dog and not knowing if it was going to pounce and attack.

"See!" glared the Sergeant, turning his back on Sylvia and gathering up some paperwork from the counter. "Nothing to worry about."

I stood, breath held, and watched Sylvia

sway back and forth. She checked us out, one by one. I watched her blood-spotted eyes slowly move from, Raven, Max, Dave, and then to me. What was going on inside that messed-up head of hers? Did she even have any knowledge of life anymore? Was she too far gone to remember who she was and how her life had once been? Was I staring at a future reflection of myself? I closed my eyes. She was what I feared for my future. Sylvia started to hum and I opened my eyes. That wide, rotten grin was still stretched across her face.

"Dave?" I whispered. "This isn't right. She should be locked up."

"I can't go against the Sergeant's orders," he whispered back. His eyes fell upon Sylvia and I could see he was thinking the same but wouldn't admit it – not in front of the Sergeant anyway. "I'm sure if she's been deemed fit by a doctor then it must be fine."

"You can leave us now." The Sergeant turned around and spoke to the two officers who had escorted Sylvia into the police station.

"Thanks, Sarge." They nodded their heads and left the room.

I counted who that left inside the custody suite. There was Grace, Dave, Eric, and the Sergeant. Was that enough to stop Sylvia Green if she suddenly woke up out of her grinning, trance-like state? No. I knew it wouldn't be. Not after witnessing Alex in the Bishop's house. How many police officers had he wiped out? I couldn't even remember. Maybe I didn't want to be remember.

Sylvia suddenly shuffled forward a few steps. I jumped. Max sprang back. She began to laugh.

"It's all right, it's okay," mumbled Dave, his hand clasped tightly around his pepper spray, which hung from his belt. "Sarge, I really think she should be restrained."

"I thought I'd made it clear who's in charge here," snapped the Sergeant.

"Sorry, Sarge," said Dave. "It's just that she could be a risk to others and herself. Whoever the doctor is that authorised her fit must have a screw loose."

The Sergeant spun around and faced Dave, obviously annoyed by the constable's interference. "I have been waiting for three months to interview this girl. She has no relatives, no known address, and right before she was arrested, a young man was seen running away from her on the Millar's Dale Bridge. I need to identify this man, as it is believed he was trying to push her off." The Sergeant took a breath before carrying on. "Every time I have called the asylum for an update, I have been told she's unfit for interview. So, when I received a call from the asylum a little before you turned up, to say she could be interviewed, I jumped at the chance and told them I would send two officers over to collect her. I'm no medical man but I trust a doctor's opinion." The Sergeant pulled a sheet of paper from out of a tray. Running his finger down the page, he stopped, "Ahh, here it is, the doctor who called was named Ben Fletcher."

CHAPTER TWENTY

My mouth dropped open. Raven, who was still standing behind me, gripped my shoulders, a gasp escaping her lips.

"Did you hear that?" she mumbled in my ear.

"Yes," I breathed, feeling slightly stunned and not quite sure what to make of the sudden announcement that had come from the Sergeant.

Max slowly sidled over to stand beside me, his watchful eyes never leaving Sylvia Green.

"I thought Ben was on our side?" he whispered. "What's going on?"

My eyes moved from the Sergeant, to Dave, and then satisfied that they were caught up in their own conversation and not listening to us, I whispered, "He is on our side." But was he? What was Ben playing at, getting Sylvia released from the asylum? How did he know we would be here, at Carden Police Station? Maybe he didn't. I shook my head, feeling deflated. What the hell was going on?

"Told you," Raven gloated. "You can't trust any of these filthy Hell worshipers! Just because he got Doshia away from us doesn't mean he's our best friend!" She leant over my shoulder so her face was just inches from mine. "He got her out so she could kill us!"

"No, that makes no sense," I argued. "If Ben wanted us dead then he could have done it already. He's had plenty of opportunities to kill us, but he hasn't."

"You wanna know what I think?" whispered Max, his eyes wide as Sylvia let out a deep chuckle. "I think we've been played – had, not only by Jude but Ben, too. Both Demons want us and both will be against each other. Somehow, this has all been planned – getting us three here with another VA drug victim. We know that we alone aren't enough for a Demon to have full control over the Cleaners – now there's four of us." He nodded his head in Sylvia's direction.

"Yes, but look at her. Can she really be good enough to house a cleaner?" I asked. "I thought that was why Middleton hadn't bothered with her – she was another failed VA experiment."

"Maybe Middleton isn't aware of Sylvia's release and still believes her to have gone crazy like the others did?" suggested Raven, still leaning over my shoulder. "The Demons are working against each other, remember? I'm pretty sure Ben hasn't told Middleton that he's just had Sylvia released. It's like a sneaky race against time to get us all together. Think about it, we're probably a Demon's wet dream, all here as a group."

"I still don't think that Ben is playing us," I whispered. "Quint, maybe. But Ben? No."

"You never thought Jude would turn out to be one of them," Raven reminded me. "But how wrong were you? You're not gonna make that same stupid mistake again, are you, and get us all killed?"

I glared at Raven. "Hey, you were fooled too!"

"Are we even sure that Jude is really a Demon?" questioned Max. "You could be wrong, Kassidy. Ben could have told you anything just to make you trust him."

"No... no, I'm sure... everything made sense. We've already gone over this," I said. "Everything points to Jude being Doshia. Haven't you noticed how since we've been apart from him there hasn't been any creepy Demon shit happening?"

"I guess," sighed Max. "But the same could be said for not having Ben with us." Max stared at me with a look of doubt.

"Jude is definitely Doshia," piped in Raven. "That I do believe!"

Our whispering was cut over by a loud wailing screech from Sylvia. She shuffled forward, arms outstretched and fingers opening and shutting like pincers.

Dave stepped forward, and using his arms to herd her back, he said to the Sergeant, "Sarge, do you want me to take this one down to the cells?" It was obvious that Dave felt uneasy having Sylvia on the loose. I couldn't blame him. Just the sight of her had the hairs on the back of my neck standing on edge. I shuddered as she snarled at me.

"In all good time," answered the Sergeant. He turned to Eric, who was now chatting to Grace over by the whiteboard. "Eric, I want you to make that call to Holly Tree Police Station. Find out what they know about these three." He opened up the flap in the counter and stepped back behind it. "Grace, have you made that call for a doctor to attend?"

"Yes, Sarge," she smiled. "But he won't be able to get here until later tonight. He's held up at Gum Brook Station."

The Sergeant tutted and then turned his attention to us. "You have the right to speak to a solicitor free of charge, read a book called Pace, Codes and Practices, and you are entitled to make a phone call. Do any of you want to do this?"

I rolled my eyes. A solicitor was not going to

be of any help – not unless he was trained in performing exorcisms. As for a phone call, we all looked at each other and shrugged. None of us had anyone to call. We were loners. All we had were each other. We shook our heads at the Sergeant.

"Very well," he said. "Dave, take them down to the cells."

"No!" Raven suddenly shouted. "You can't lock us away! We need to go. Haven't you listened to a word we've said? That fog will get here soon. You're all in danger!"

"Do you really think I'm just going to let three people arrested on suspicion of murder walk free?" The Sergeant frowned.

"We didn't murder anyone!" shouted Max. "And if you make that phone call to Holly Tree Police Station then you've just signed our death warrants."

The Sergeant waved his hands in the air as if to brush us away. "I've heard enough. Take them down, Dave."

"No, I'm not going!" shouted Raven, she kicked out at Dave as he tried to restrain her.

"You're just going to make this harder on yourself," Dave grunted, trying to get a hold of Raven. "Listen to me! Nothing's going to happen to you. You're quite safe here at the station. I promise you!"

"No, we're not," hissed Raven.

"Dave, I've got someone else being brought in," glared the Sergeant. "I want this custody suite cleared."

I grabbed hold of Raven's hand. "I don't want to be put in a cell either, but if you don't go quietly they're gonna put you back in handcuffs."

"Listen to your mate," puffed Dave, finally in control of the situation.

Raven pulled away from Dave. She glared out from under her hair. "Fine!" she snapped, folding her arms tightly about her.

I took one more look over at Sylvia. Her coat had been removed and her bare arms were riddled with a weave of black veins. She saw me watching her. Her crazy eyes lit up and she flexed her hands, stretching out her fingers. I recoiled at the sight of them. She had no fingernails, just bloodied stumps. Had the asylum removed them?

"My meds are dead... I'm waking up!" she spluttered, like her throat was filled with bile.

"What did she say?" asked Eric, pushing Max forward towards a cell door.

"Fuck knows," answered Dave. "Maybe the asylum has had her on some kind of drug... you know... something that keeps her calm. Maybe it's running out?"

I looked at Raven and Max. I didn't fancy being around Sylvia if the effects of her medication was running low. What would she be like without it? I shuddered at the thought. Part of me was relieved to be going into the cells out of her reach, even though I knew we would be trapped when the Cleaners caught up with us.

CHAPTER TWENTY ONE

"Right, this way," Dave ordered. He had opened up a door and was now waiting for us to follow him. He took us through another door and into the cells. It was a room with a central corridor and the cells ran along both sides. They were each sectioned off with bars, allowing me to see into each of them. Cell number 8 was occupied by a man sleeping on a bunk. The rest were empty. The rattle of keys echoed through the room as Dave opened up cell five.

He gestured to Max. "You're in here."

Max walked in and stood behind the bars. Dave locked him in. I watched as cell six was opened.

"In you go," said Dave, holding out his arm like he was inviting us into his home. Raven stomped in and slumped down onto the bunk. I followed her in and turned to look at Dave.

"How long will it be before the doctor sees us?" I asked, feeling suddenly anxious at being trapped inside this cell. Time was an issue for us and I knew we probably didn't have long before the Cleaners showed up.

"Could be a couple of hours, maybe longer,"

answered Dave. "Someone will be along soon with something to eat." He turned the key in the lock and started to walk away.

I walked over to the bars which joined the cell that Max was in. He pushed his hair from out of his face and gave me a half-hearted smile.

"Not sure how we're gonna get out of this," he said, clinging onto one of the bars. He looked about. "There's no way out except the way we came in. These windows are too narrow, and besides that, the glass is covered with bars. We're trapped." He walked over to the cell door and gave it a tug. Looking back at me, he said, "That was my brother they were talking about. It has to be. But I don't believe for one minute that Robert was trying to push Sylvia off that bridge. Why would he? He escaped with her, got her to the Bishop's, and got as far as we have. Why would he try to kill her?"

"They've got it wrong, Max," I said. "Maybe from a distance that's how it looked. It's easy to misread a situation if you're not a part of it. Robert was probably trying to stop her from jumping." I looked away from his stare. I didn't want to tell him that maybe Robert had tried to kill her. There was every chance that Max's brother could be just like Alex and Sylvia. I feared that if I told Max this, then he would just give up.

"At least we know Robert is alive," mumbled Raven, peering around the cell. "This cellblock is creepy, don't you think?"

I stared up at the ceiling. The lights were pretty dim, casting the cells in an eerie glow. Looking up at the small square window I could see the daylight was beginning to fade. I climbed up onto the bunk, and standing on tiptoes, I peered out through the window. Tiny splatters of rain had started to fall and the wind had picked up. At least there were no signs of fog.

"We've got to think of a way out of here," I said, climbing off the bunk.

"Well there's no point in us being sent to the asylum now," grumbled Raven. "Not now that Sylvia's here." She stood up. "We need to escape with Sylvia and take her to Doctor Langstone's."

"What? Have you lost your mind?" said Max. "She's deranged. She'll kill us before we even get outside this police station."

"But she's obviously wanted by the Demons. If Ben Fletcher thinks she's good enough for a Cleaner then..." she trailed off. "Why else did Ben get her released? Probably because he wants us all to himself but if we keep her and get your brother, then we're harder for them to take. We'll be stronger together than apart. Think of Sylvia like a bit of a guard dog. We let her loose when the Demons come for us. She'll rip them apart if she's anything like Alex was."

"You can't use people like that!" I glared. "It's wrong."

"Is it?" snapped Raven. "It's only what's happened to us! We've all been used and abused. Let someone else get it for once instead of us always being the target. I nearly got stabbed to death on that train, and as if that wasn't bad enough, I almost got run down by a bloody train." Raven paced up and down, her face like thunder. "Sylvia's had it easy tucked away out of sight in that asylum while we've been chased, lied to, and attacked. Let Sylvia get some of the action – she won't get hurt. She's probably a lot stronger than us."

"You're crazy," I said, shaking my head.

"No, I just want to survive – I want to win for once!" Raven sighed, slumping back down onto the bunk.

I looked at Max. "You don't agree with this, do you?"

"Not with using Sylvia as a punching bag, no." Max shook his head. "But if there is a way of taking her with us, then I think we should."

I gasped, surprised by Max's sudden change

of mind. "But you said yourself that she's deranged!"

"I know, but... if Robert tried to take her with him then I think I should try."

"How?" I asked. "I admire your good will, Max, really I do, but how can we take someone along with us who might kill us?"

"I don't know," shrugged Max. "I just feel like she's one of us and needs our help."

I clung onto the bars with both hands and rested my head against the cold metal. The whole idea seemed insane. We were already up to our necks in it, why add more baggage? But however much I argued about this, inside my head, that little part of me, the one that told me right from wrong, nibbled away at my heart. Sylvia was still human. Somewhere deep inside her – the real Sylvia – still existed. Alex had showed me that. How would I feel if I was left behind? If I became like her, would I want to be disowned? Left to the mercy of god-knows-what? But still, I just couldn't see a way of taking her with us and keeping the rest of us safe.

"Look, if you can think of a plausible and safe way of taking Sylvia then I'm all ears," I said. "But before we can even consider such a thing, we need to be coming up with ideas of how to get out of this cell." I shook the bars and they clanged loudly. The sound of keys suddenly jangled and the door to the cellblock opened. I peered through the bars and saw Eric stroll in, Sylvia shuffling behind him, followed by Dave. They walked her down and stopped in front of cell 7. I watched her closely. On first appearance, she appeared to be nothing more than someone who had lost their mind – oblivious to what was going on around her. But as I stared closely at Sylvia, I could see she was taking everything in. Her bloodied eyes twitched from left to right. It was like she was checking out every little detail – storing information. But why? For what reason? I shuddered as she turned her head. Those eyes of hers stared back at me.

"Come on," said Eric, prodding Sylvia in the back. "In you go." He shut the gate on her. "That's another fucked-up smack-head locked away."

Dave was quick to turn the key in the lock. I smiled to myself as I heard him let out a sigh. *You should be afraid,* I thought to myself, *afraid of what's to come.*

"Take a good look!" laughed Eric, coming to stand beside our cells. "That is what you're gonna become. Dumb kids! Think you can just jack-up and kill a bunch of people! Well I guess that's gonna be your punishment." He laughed again.

"Enough, Eric," Dave barked.

"Yeah, why don't you just fuck off, pig!" hissed Raven, coming to stand beside me. "You'll get yours – just you wait and see!"

"Yeah?" snapped Eric. "And you're gonna give it to me, are ya? From behind those bars?" He laughed again. "Not so able-bodied now, are ya, locked in there?"

I could feel myself knotting up. Anger seemed to consume me like a raging bull. Right now I wanted nothing more than to rip his fucking head off. "You're so fucking blind!" I sneered from behind the bars. "Laugh it up, you arrogant twat, because when we get out of here, we're gonna come and find you and I'm gonna rip that ugly little grin from your face!" I lunged at the bars causing them to rattle. Eric jumped back.

Regaining his composure, and acting like he hadn't been frightened, Eric glared at me. "You're nothing but a dirty little skanky bitch who would drop her knickers for anyone as long as they had drugs."

"Eric!" shouted Dave. "Leave it, will you? Enough!"

I stood my ground and smiled back at Eric. His words meant nothing. They couldn't hurt me. There was a lot worse out there than people like Eric. I knew it. Soon, he would, too.

CHAPTER TWENTY TWO

The cellblock fell silent. Dave and Eric had left. I felt the anger drain from me as quickly as it had started.

"That guy's a knob!" said Max, peering at me through the bars.

I nodded my head in agreement and looked down at my black veins. It had to be this stuff in me that caused my anger. I was never someone who just lost it before. It kind of made sense, really. After all, I had some kind of Demon stuff in me – Demons weren't nice, they were kind of angry. So didn't it make sense that I would feel their emotions – behave like them?

"Umm, Kassidy!" I heard Max whisper.

"What?" I looked up at him. Max had his face pressed against the bars, his eyes wide.

He tipped his head back as if to use it to point me in the right direction. "Behind me."

Sylvia. I had forgotten she was in here, what, with the row that had just taken place. I peered over Max's shoulder. "She's just standing by the bars staring at us," I whispered.

"Say something to her," mumbled Raven, standing behind me. "Go on!"

I looked past Max again. Sylvia hadn't moved. Her eyes seemed to penetrate right through me. I shivered and shot a sideways glance at Raven. "You say something," I pushed. "You want to take her with us – it should be you who tries to communicate with her."

"Hi, Sylvia," whispered Raven, forcing a smile which looked more like a grimace. Raven didn't do smiling well. "Are... you all right?"

Silence. Sylvia made no response.

"Try again," Max said, still not looking at Sylvia.

"You're Sylvia... right? Do you want to know my name?" asked Raven.

There was no reply. The only sound in the cellblock was the splatters of rain hitting the windows.

"Great," whispered Max. "I'm not sure I can spend a night here with her just standing at the bars staring at us."

"Me neither," I agreed. I glanced back at Sylvia. She hadn't moved an inch. Her arms hung loosely by her sides and her head drooped slightly to the right. If her feet hadn't been firmly on the floor, she would have looked like she was hanging.

"Ask her something else," pushed Max, still looking into our cell, afraid to look at Sylvia.

I took a deep breath and peered through the bars and into Sylvia's cell. "Sylvia... do you remember what happened to you at Cruor Pharma?"

A sudden gust of wind had the rain pelting against the windows, but Sylvia remained quiet.

I looked at Max and Raven and shrugged my shoulders.

"It's no use," sighed Max. "She's like brain-dead. We'll never get any information out of her."

I wasn't so sure. As I stared at Sylvia, I felt certain that there was something behind those menacing eyes of hers. A twitch – a small flicker had caught my attention as I'd mentioned Cruor Pharma.

"Do you remember Robert O'Brien?" asked Raven. "He helped you to escape?"

I watched Sylvia's reaction closely. She stood motionless, yet there it was again – a faint movement of her pupils at hearing Robert's name. I lifted both arms and waved them franticly at her. She didn't flinch.

"Sylvia, do you remember Alex?" Raven quizzed.

There it was again. Another movement of her eyes. I turned away from her and whispered, "She knows more than she's letting on. I can see it in her eyes. What I don't know, though, is whether she's keeping quiet deliberately. Maybe she doesn't trust us? Perhaps she's playing at being crazy – you know, to keep herself safe. After all, it's kept her out of the hands of Doctor Middleton for the past three months. Could it all be just an act?"

"It's a bloody good act!" whispered Max, through the bars. "She's got me well and truly believing." He shivered and rubbed his hands up and down his arms. "Trouble is, I'm not sure if I want to test the waters! I don't fancy entering the lion's den in the hope that I won't get my head bitten off!"

"The only other scenario is that she's completely deranged from the VA10 or..." I trailed off, suddenly feeling very cold. A disturbing thought had entered my head.

"Or what?" hissed Raven impatiently.

"Or... she might have a Demon inside her," I whispered, feeling a chill run up my spine. "It's possible. We know there are lone Demons out there – not just the ones from Cruor Pharma."

"Well that's it then," sighed Max. "We can't possibly risk taking her with us." He looked disappointed – or was it relief? I couldn't tell.

"No... we have to take her," insisted Raven. She glared at Max. "Stick your finger through the bars and see what she does!"

"What?" said Max, his eyes wide. "I'm not sticking my fingers through there or anything else."

"It's the only way we're gonna find out if she's friendly or not," spat Raven. "Kassidy and I can't do it. Your cell is next to hers. Only you can reach her."

We all turned round, each of us flinching. Sylvia was now pressed up tight against the bars, her fingers wrapped firmly around them. That same piercing stare lingered in her eyes. Had she been listening to us? She had crept up against Max's cell without us hearing her, like an animal stalking its prey. We jumped at the sound of rain hitting the window hard, but not Sylvia. Nothing seemed to stir her.

"Well?" Raven asked. "Go on, now's your chance." She placed her hand through the bars into Max's cell and gripped onto his arm. "Do it now while she's pressed up against the bars."

"No way!" said Max, refusing to move.

"We need to know before we get a chance of escaping out of here," pushed Raven. "As soon as we get a chance to run we don't want to be pondering – should we or shouldn't we let her out. Decisions need to be made now. You never know how soon our chance of escape will be!"

"Wait!" I whispered. "You can't make Max stick his fingers in there. You wouldn't do it!"

"Would you?" snapped Raven, her eyes narrowed into slits.

"No, I wouldn't," I argued. "I'm not fucking suicidal and neither is Max!"

"Fine!" huffed Raven, folding her arms across her chest. "We'll just wait here and fuck-up our escape when the time is right!" She turned her back on us.

I looked at Max. He stared down at his feet.

"It's okay, Max," I said softly, slipping my arm through the bars and taking his hand in mine. "I think it's a dumb idea – a dangerous one at that." I looked at Sylvia and shuddered. She still clung onto the bars and watched silently, only now she had pushed her face right up to the bars so it was half-pushed between the rows of metal. It looked scrunched up like it had been trapped in a set of lift doors.

"It's not okay," said Max, pulling his hand away. "I want to find out about Robert. I want to help Sylvia like my brother had... but..." He stopped mid-sentence and looked down at his black fingernails. "But... I guess I'm not as brave as Robert."

"You need to be like a bloody gladiator not

to be afraid of that!" I said, looking at Sylvia. "There aren't many who would enter the arena with her standing inside!"

"My brother did!" whispered Max, still staring at his fingernails. "I wish I was as strong as him."

"You are," I argued. "Stop thinking like that."

Max shook his head. "No – Robert's always been the stronger out of the two of us. It was him giving himself up for a drug trial to get us some money – not me!"

"It was you who put yourself up for one so you could find him," I said. "That's brave! You knew there was something wrong at Cruor Pharma, yet it didn't stop you from going in search of Robert."

Max took in a deep breath then let out a slow sigh. "I just feel fucking useless, Kassidy. Look at me! I can't even poke a finger through those bars over there without getting shit-scared!" He dropped his head down, his long, blonde hair draped over the side of his pale face.

"Max," I whispered. "We're all shit-scared – who wouldn't be?" I looked up at the window as the rain continued to fall. "But we can't give up. Yeah – we're stuck in a hole at the moment but we'll get out – I know we will. We have to. The

Cleaners, Cropper, and now Jude are all after us. We've got two choices – we can get out of this cell and run... or we can lay down on these shit bunks and wait for them to come get us!" I felt my heart sink at the mention of Jude. I still felt cheated – deceived. And a part of me felt sad. Sad because I had liked Jude. Sad because a part of our group had fallen away, leaving now just the three of us. But I also felt scared. I had seen what Doshia was capable of and if he ever got inside one of us then... I shuddered.

"Hey, pretty lady!"

I looked up. The voice had come from the man locked up in cell 8. He staggered over to the bars which adjoined Sylvia's cell.

"Hey, lady in the gown," he slurred.

I looked at Sylvia. Was she going to respond? No. She still had her face pushed between the two bars, staring at us.

"Hey!" shouted the man, rattling on the bars. "I'm talking to you!"

"Piss-head!" moaned Raven, coming over to stand beside me.

"I wouldn't talk to her if I was you," called out Max. "She's not right!"

"Ya bird, is she?" laughed the man. "Well... she might wanna talk with me!" He yanked on the bars again, filling the cellblock with echoes of clanging metal.

"Oh – what's ya name, blondie?!"

"Listen," began Max, peering through the bars to get a better look at the drunk.

"No!" piped in Raven, grabbing hold of Max's arm. She pulled him up against the bars. "Let him!"

"What?" I gasped. "He's just a drunk – he doesn't deserve to get attacked by Sylvia!" I suddenly had painful images of my dad floating before me. Just because people had a drinking problem, didn't mean that they were disposable – that they didn't count.

"We need to know what she's capable of," snapped Raven. "Max won't do it so let him."

The cellblock suddenly filled again with clanging metal. The drunk pressed his body up against the bars and continued to call out to Sylvia.

"Stop!" I shouted, looking from the drunk and then at Sylvia. "Please... don't do it... you'll get hurt."

"Listen," hissed Raven, "It's us against everyone else. You wanna get out of here? Then stop thinking about everyone who doesn't matter and start thinking about our survival. If she attacks him then we'll know for sure that we can't take her. If she doesn't then we're safe to let her come with us!"

"Blondie – blondie!" the man hollered, swinging on the bars.

I held my hands up to my face. "This is so wrong!"

"No, it's called looking after number one!" spat Raven. "If she attacks him then the police will come in. That will be our chance to get out of these cells." Raven stared out from under her hair. "I'll play dead or something – you call them over. When they open up – you attack them!" She looked at me, her eyes almost as crazy as Sylvia's.

I looked to Max. Did he think this was a good idea? He seemed stunned by the very thought.

"Max?" I stared at him through the bars.

"I'm not sure this is gonna work... or if I even want to watch that drunk get assaulted," said Max. "I was kinda hoping that I'd left all that shit behind."

"Hey... sweetheart!" The drunk shook the bars again. "Come and chat with me... it's lonely over 'ere!"

We stood, breath held. I hoped that Sylvia would take no notice of him. I waited, frozen to the spot. Time seemed to slow. I found myself wishing that the drunk would just give up and move away from harm's reach. The tension growing inside the cellblock filled me with dread. I didn't want to see any more death. After what seemed like forever, I felt myself relax a little. Sylvia had paid no attention to the drunk man whatsoever. As I let out a deep sigh, relieved that nothing terrible had happened, the drunk called out again.

"Hey! Blondie, what ya doing in that hospital gown... come 'ere... I'll give ya a kiss better." He sniggered, pushing both arms through the bars and wiggling them about.

All of a sudden, Sylvia pulled away from where she had been standing. She turned around and faced the drunk. Her steps were stiff as she shuffled towards the drunk's outstretched arms.

"No!" I shouted. "Move your arms – get away from her!" I clung onto the bars and shook them. "She'll kill you!" I watched in fear as Sylvia staggered over. Couldn't the drunk see what she looked like now that she was facing him? Didn't he see her bloody eyes – her black veins, and rotten, stumpy teeth? "Move – move!" I screamed at the top of my voice. "Max – stop him – tell him to get away!"

Max suddenly leapt over to the bars adjoining Sylvia's cell and gripped them tightly. He shook them, filling the cellblock with a thunderous clanging boom. "Get back!" hollered Max. "Move away!"

Raven stood and smiled.

I threw my hands up to my face. My body trembled. I stared in horror as Sylvia reached the drunk.

CHAPTER TWENTY THREE

Before the drunk man realised what was happening, Sylvia had snatched hold of his arms. The man's body hit the bars at speed as she yanked him forward. His face hit the metal so hard that you could see an indentation running vertically down from the top of his forehead to his chin. Sylvia wrenched him forward again. The clang of metal and the crunch of bones filled my ears. Within seconds, the man's nose was flattened to a bloody pulp. Blood poured down his chin and into his mouth as he opened it to scream.

"Stop it!" I yelled. "Stop it, Sylvia!" I pulled on my cell door, hoping the noise would alert the police officers. Surely they could hear all this turmoil? The drunk was screaming, the bars clanging, Max and me shouting and... I stopped. A chill ran up my spine. A deep cackle filled the room. I turned my head slowly, almost afraid to look. Sylvia was laughing. Her head snapped round and she grinned at me from under her matted hair. Her black, stumpy teeth chatted together like she was out in the cold. She jerked backwards again and again, still hanging onto the drunk man's wrists. His face pounded and pounded into the bars until it looked no more than a bloody mush of flesh.

"Please... help us!" Max shouted.

Sylvia cackled again. She lunged forward and ripped into the man's arm, her black teeth sinking deeply into him. I felt my stomach lurch as a lump of flesh was torn free and swung about from between the rotted stumps in her mouth. She stretched open her lips and gulped the flesh down – swallowing it whole. The man slumped down to his knees, still pressed up tight against the bars. A whimper escaped his mouth. Sylvia dropped to the floor. She snatched at his hair and pulled his head forward. I heard the man squeal as she bit into his face.

"For fuck's sake!" screamed Max, pounding his fists against the metal bars. "Help!"

As if in response to Max's cries, Sylvia jumped up, a handful of flesh grasped tightly between her fingers. She flung the bloodied mess through the bars into the cell that Max occupied and stood swaying on her feet. Her arms now hung loosely again by her sides – her head drooping again to the right. She stared – a bloodied grin across her face.

Max stepped aside, away from the flesh, which had landed near his feet. It lay splattered over the floor, bits of it stuck to the bars and slowly slithered down the metal.

The doors to the cellblock suddenly flew open. Dave walked through.

"What's all the commotion about...?" he grumbled, his eyes searching each cell. He gasped – took a few steps back as the carnage in cell 7 and 8 became apparent. "What the hell...!" He staggered forward and gripped hold of the bars to support himself. Reaching for his radio, his voice trembled. "Eric, call an ambulance – there's been an incident down in the cellblock. That nutter from the asylum is all bloodied–up and the man in cell 8 looks like he's been through a blender – hurry!"

He reached for his keys and headed for cell 7.

"No!" I screeched. "Don't open up that one. Cell 8... that man is the victim... not her!" I could feel myself shake. My stomach still churned. I stepped over to the bars and peered through, hoping that the drunk was still alive. He lay still, sprawled out on his back. His face, or what was left of it, looked like a regurgitated mess of Bolognese and jelly. I wanted to vomit. "Is he still alive?"

Dave didn't answer. He was on his hands and knees. I glared at Raven. She stood beside me, watching Sylvia.

"This is your fault," I spat.

"How?" scowled Raven. "It wasn't me in there ripping that pisshead to shreds."

"No, but it's what you wanted," I snapped. "You were quite happy to watch that man like he was nothing but a guinea pig in an experiment. After what happened to you in Cruor Pharma – I can't believe you would be happy to let that happen." I peered back through the bars. Dave was still down on his knees.

"Well?" whispered Raven. "Are we going to stick to the plan or what?"

"What plan?" I snapped.

"Me pretending to be dead or something, and you calling that police officer over – now's the perfect time." Raven stood with her hands on her hips.

"That was never my plan," I glared. "That was your sick, fucked-up idea. Do you really think he's gonna come running over here when he's got that mess to sort out?" I turned away from Raven and looked at Max. He was leaning up against the bars. His face was pale.

"Max, you okay?" I asked, reaching through the bars and gently running my fingers down his arm. I knew it was a stupid question to ask after what had just happened, but what else could I say?

"We have to get out of here," he

whispered. "We have to get VA20 out of us. I don't want to end up like her." He glanced up at Sylvia, who still stood swaying on her feet.

"We won't be like her," I said. Even as the words escaped my lips, I doubted them myself. "We're not like her or Alex."

"They've had three months to become that," whispered Max. "We've only had VA20 in us for a short time – I already feel different – you know what I mean. You said yourself that you didn't like the way it made you feel. We're changing, Kassidy, slowly, but it's happening." He took hold of my hand and squeezed it. "Maybe Robert did try to push Sylvia off that bridge... and you know what? I don't think I can blame him."

Eric strolled into the cellblock. He took one look into cell 8 and stood just outside the door. "Jeez, what the hell happened?"

"I don't know, but he needs an ambulance." Dave stood up. His hands were covered in blood and the knees of his trousers were wet through.

"The ambulance is on its way," frowned Eric, cautiously looking into Sylvia's cell. "That freak should have never been let out of the asylum. The Sarge is pulling his hair out in custody – swearing all sorts about the doctor who allowed her out."

"Someone's gonna get their collar felt for

this," said Dave. "And it ain't gonna be me."

"I told you – I warned you about her!" I shouted, angry that they hadn't listened.

Eric strolled towards my cell. He glared at me and said, "Of course, you'd know all about this, you filthy crackhead. How you can just stand there after what you lot got up to on that train? You're worse than her."

"Whatever!" sneered Raven. "When we get out of here..."

"When you get out of here – it's gonna be in the back of another police van," Eric grinned. "Inspector Cropper was very interested to hear that you lot were locked up in Carden. He's on his way right now." Eric stood with his arms folded, a smug look across his face. "Seen any more fog?" He turned his back on us and laughed.

"See!" huffed Raven. "We should've gone with my plan. We might have been out of these cells by now."

"No, we wouldn't," glared Max. He turned towards the door that led into the cellblock. Two paramedics holding a stretcher had walked in. They went into cell 8 and crouched down over the drunk man. I turned away and climbed up onto the bunk. The rain still fell hard against the window. At least there was still no sign of any fog. But did that matter now? Inspector Cropper was on his way. Whichever got us first, we would still end up back inside Cruor Pharma – unless Doshia got here before them. I wondered about Ben. What had happened to him after we had separated along the train tracks? Fears of him being killed by Doshia had gone now, after knowing that it had been Ben who had called the Sarge about releasing Sylvia from the asylum. It meant that he was still alive. But why had he got Sylvia released? Did he know something about her that we didn't? As far as I could see, she was nothing but a crazy killer. Not someone who Middleton would call a breakthrough for his drug trials. She was already fucked up. What would a cleaner inside her make her become? But there had to be something about Sylvia. Even if it had been Quint who had got her released, she had to be important in all this mess somehow.

    I stepped off the bunk and joined Raven and Max at the cell bars. The drunk man was carried away on the stretcher out of the cellblock. I could hear Dave and Eric talking quietly.

    "Where's the Sarge?" asked Dave. "Why isn't he down here?"

    "He's booking in another prisoner," answered Eric, peering through the bars at Sylvia.

"What about her? We're gonna have to move her out of that cell and put her in a clean one. The floor's covered in blood and so is she. Complaints and discipline are going to have a fucking fit when they see this shit. We need to get this sorted."

Dave scratched his head. "I know, but there's only us two available at the moment."

"What about me?" called Max. "My cell has blood in it too, I'm not staying in this one. I want to be moved."

Dave walked over to Max's cell. Seeing the blood splattered over the floor, he said, "Okay, I'll move you in a minute."

Max turned and winked at me. I knew what he had planned. But could Max pull it off?

CHAPTER TWENTY FOUR

A call came over Dave's radio. Its static hissed and echoed through the cellblock.

"You and Eric are needed up in Custody," the voice hissed through the radio. It was the Sergeant. "Have you cleaned up that mess yet?"

"No, Sarge," answered Dave, rolling his eyes at Eric.

"Leave that for the moment," ordered the Sergeant. "I have a prisoner ready to be taken to the cells. You can clear up that mess after."

Dave spoke into his radio again. "Shouldn't we contact complaints and discipline? They're gonna need to…"

"Just get your arse back here and stop questioning my orders!" the sergeant barked via the radio.

Dave rolled his eyes again. "On our way."

"For fuck's sake!" moaned Eric. "When is the next shift on? I've had enough of this bullshit for one day." He looked at his watch. "I still haven't had any grub yet and we still have to travel back from this shit-hole of a station."

"Let's just get on with it," said Dave, looking back at Max. "You – stay away from those bars – I don't need another incident down here." He took a quick look at Sylvia and then turned and left the cellblock with Eric.

As soon as they were out of earshot, Max turned and whispered, "When that copper called Dave takes me out of this cell, I'm gonna push him into the one he's intending for me. I'll take his keys and lock him in – then I'll get you two out."

He looked nervous. I could see in his eyes that he was going over the plan inside his head. Could he do it? What if Eric came back with Dave? Could Max fight off two police officers?

"You'll need to get Dave's radio off him too," I whispered, my eyes flicking from Max over to Sylvia. She had shuffled back over to the bars adjoining Max's cell. Was she listening to our plan? Did she understand? Was there any reasoning left inside her?

"If Eric comes back you're gonna have to push them both inside." Raven crouched down slightly so she could whisper to us. Her tall, scrawny frame shadowed both Max and me.

"Do you think you can do it?" I asked.

"I have to," whispered Max. "You heard what Eric said. Inspector Cropper is on his way." He let out a deep sigh, running his hands through his hair. Rolling his shoulders back, he stood up straight as if preparing himself for the fight. "When we get out, we head back to custody, through the doors, and down the corridor we first came in by."

"Then what?" asked Raven.

"We run," I hushed, ever aware that Sylvia was listening to us. "We run and we find somewhere to hide – until it all dies down. Then we find a way to Doctor Langstone's. It can't be too far from here."

"What about our stuff?" whispered Raven. "I want that jacket back. I'm not running around wearing this flower-power blouse so everyone can laugh at me."

"I don't give a shit about your blouse," I said, "But I do want the satchel back. Father Williams' diary is in there, the iPod, and the rosary beads."

"And the two passports," said Max. "I would like my brother's passport. It's the only picture I have of him now. Well, apart from the ones I have back in Holly Tree, but who knows if we'll ever get back there."

"What about Sylvia?" asked Raven. "Are we leaving her here?"

"You really need to ask that?" said Max, his eyes wide.

"I know it's crazy – she's crazy, but I just

don't think we should leave her here." Raven stared at us with her dark eyes.

"Why?" questioned Max, screwing his nose up at the idea.

"Hold on," I cut across them both. "I've been kind of thinking along the same lines." I looked at Max. "I know it's crazy, and I've no idea of how we can do it without Sylvia trying to kill us, but I have this nagging feeling in me that she's important somehow. If we leave her here then Middleton gets his hands on her."

"Don't you mean Ben?" questioned Max. "It was him, after all, who got her released to this police station."

"I still believe in Ben, however mad that may seem, but I don't think he's against us – he had her released for a reason. I don't know what that is but... he must think that Sylvia holds some relevance in all this."

"But how can we take her?" pushed Max. "She's insane!"

"The Demons want her – that's her relevance!" hissed Raven. "But why let them have her? Why give them something they want which ultimately will harm us if they get their filthy satanic hands on her. I say we keep her – us against them!" Raven crossed her arms, a determined look in her eyes. She stared at Max, knowing that he was the one who needed to be pushed into agreeing. "We'll whack a pair of handcuffs on her or something."

"This idea is as insane as Sylvia is," whispered Max, shaking his head.

"It probably is..." I agreed. "But..."

The doors to the cellblock suddenly opened. We turned around and saw Dave walk in. I felt my mouth drop open as my eyes fell upon his prisoner.

CHAPTER TWENTY FIVE

We stared wide-eyed in silence. What little colour Max and Raven had in their faces drained away. I was sure mine had done the same. I suddenly felt shaky. I could feel my legs tremble. I gripped hold of the bars and watched Dave unlock the cell opposite mine and Raven's.

"In you go," ordered Dave, gesturing with his hands.

Jude strolled in. The cell door was locked behind him and he turned around. His eyes met mine and I looked away. I held my hand up to my chest, my heart thumping wildly. From the corner of my eye, I saw Max back away from his cell door. How did we play this? Did Jude know of our suspicions? But if he didn't — should we act like we didn't know who he truly was? Just so he wouldn't attack us — take us for his soon-to-be servants — the Cleaners. But if he did know, what were his intentions? He had us in the perfect setting. Locked in these cells — unable to escape. I looked at Sylvia. He had her now also. Were we enough — all four bodies for the Cleaners to dwell in? Was Jude just going to sit this out — wait for the Cleaners to arrive? I turned away from him. My head was in a muddle. How did he even get himself arrested? He must have deliberately given himself up – just so he could catch up with us. I felt my heart pick up pace. That awful sensation of VA20 pushing through my veins had started up again – turning my stomach. Ben? What about Ben? What had he done to him? If Jude was here – then that only meant one thing. Jude – or should I say Doshia – must have killed him. Taken away the only thing that had kept Ben going for all these years – his body – leaving Quint with nothing. I closed my eyes. I didn't want to think about it. Ben had allowed us to escape from Doshia – died in the process – and now here we all were again. And for what? Nothing. But was that right? Hadn't the Sergeant said he'd received a call from Ben Fletcher only a short while ago? Could Ben still be alive?

"I'll be back in ten minutes," I heard Dave call out to Max as he left the cellblock and closed the door.

Get it together, I said to myself. See what Jude's reaction is first before you fall apart. I took a deep breath and spun around to face him. Our eyes met.

"How fucking lucky is this, eh?" Jude's face broke out into a grin, he rubbed his hands together like he'd won the lottery. "Back together again – just how we should be."

I hesitated. Was he for real? Did he really think that all was okay between us? Did he really not know that we believed him to be Doshia? Was this all an act? I really didn't have a clue. I decided to play along. Glancing quickly at Raven and winking, I forced a smile at Jude and said, "I can't believe it. Where did they pick you up?"

"Not too far from where we got separated," grinned Jude. His eyes darted to the left and fell upon Sylvia. "Who the fuck is that? That's not... you know... that girl from the passport, is it? The one you took from Ward 1?"

I nodded my head slowly. Still unsure of Jude.

"She looks a fucking mess," said Jude. "I hope your brother don't look like that." He peered through the bars at Max.

There was an uncomfortable silence. I stared from Raven to Max. By the look on their faces, neither one seemed to know how to take the sudden appearance of Jude.

"We have to get away from him," hushed Raven, suddenly standing behind me, leaning into my ear.

I pushed her away slightly. I didn't want to

alert Jude to our doubts.

"What happened to Ben?" I asked.

"I don't really know." Jude's eyes narrowed. "He started acting all funny – you know – Demon-like. The police turned up and Ben fucked off. Who knows where he went. Probably back to Cruor Pharma."

My feelings of distrust raged up inside me. I opened my mouth to say something but shut it quickly before I said anything I would regret. Jude's eyes told me nothing. They were the same as always. That same look of, 'trust me', that he had so well deceived us with. His laid-back demeanour was still present. He made the perfect 'wolf in sheep's clothing'. I didn't know whether to believe him about Ben or not. It was plausible, after all, that Quint had come forward and taken over Ben and disappeared back to Cruor Pharma. It had happened before.

"So, what's the plan, then?" smiled Jude, holding onto the bars of his cell.

"There is no plan," hissed Raven, stepping forward and glaring at Jude.

I snatched hold of Raven's arm. "I'll handle this."

She pulled away from my grip, skulking over to where Max leant up against the bars.

"What's her problem?" asked Jude. He held his hand up to stop me from answering. "Don't tell me – there is no plan because Raven doesn't have the aid of the tarot cards." He smirked at me.

"Max is being moved out of his cell into another one," I said, reluctant to tell him, but I didn't see what else I could say. "He's going to attack the police officer – get the keys – push him into the cell and lock him in."

"Then what?" asked Jude.

"Then we get the hell out of here!" I glanced at Max and Raven. They looked as on edge as I felt. Not only was the thought of escaping the police station eating up my insides, but now I had Jude-Doshia to escape from again. I had no idea how we were gonna pull that one off. I took a sneaky side-glance at Jude. He stood, eyes wandering about the cellblock. His black trousers and smart blue shirt not an inch out of place. Not like, Raven, Max, and me – dishevelled and dirty. I wanted to tell him I knew. Knew what he was – that he couldn't fool me anymore with his suggestions of going on the run together and having fun. That I wouldn't be sucked in anymore with his, 'I'll look after you' lies. But I couldn't. It was too risky. After seeing what Doshia could be capable of – making someone throw themselves to their death – get under the skin of large groups of people and turn them into crazy killers, I knew that if I wanted to stay safe – keep Raven and Max safe – then I had to play along with his deceit. At least for now.

    I began to pace up and down my cell. How much longer would Dave be? How much time did we have to make our escape before Inspector Cropper arrived? Or would it be the Cleaners who came first? I climbed back up onto the bunk. It was dark outside and the rain still fell in sheets but I couldn't see any fog. Maybe the Cleaners wouldn't come. It would make more sense to just send Inspector Cropper to come and get us. Middleton was probably still hoping to cover this all up, which he couldn't if he used the Cleaners. There were too many people about for the Cleaners to go unnoticed. Inspector Cropper looked more legit.

    I felt the bunk wobble as Raven joined me at the small cell window. She whispered in my ear. "I don't like playing along in this sham." She gazed out into the wet evening. Her long, twisted nails clattered against the glass along with the thrumming of the rain.

    "Me neither," I spoke quietly. "I really don't know what to do other than act dumb to his pretence."

"We could leave him locked up – when we get out – just leave him behind," mumbled Raven.

"You think that a locked cell door will keep Doshia away from us?" I raised my eyes. Was Raven really that slow? "He could get out of there right now if he chose to. He could open up all our cells and let us out without a key. But he won't, not while he has to keep up his act in front of us. Remember, Doshia won't reveal himself until he has enough bodies for the Cleaners. He's gonna want to keep us in the dark so he can manipulate – pull our strings – until he has us where he wants us."

"And where is that?" whispered Raven.

I checked over my shoulder to make sure that Jude wasn't watching us. Satisfied that his attention seemed to be on Sylvia, I turned and said quietly, "There's four of us here – I know Sylvia doesn't seem right but I think she will do – that's why Ben had her released. Not for his own purposes but to get her away from harm. You, Max, me, and Sylvia. Only I don't think that's enough bodies. I think Doshia is holding out for one more." My eyes met Raven's. The darkness in her pupils almost seemed to light up as the penny dropped.

"Robert," she mumbled under her breath.

"Jude's gonna want to keep lying until we get to Doctor Langstone's and find Robert. I think that's his plan, anyway."

"He never wanted to go to Doctor Langstone's though," quizzed Raven.

"Not until he heard for sure from the Bishop that Robert and Sylvia had headed there. Remember when we first found Father Williams' diary? It was written that he suggested that they should head to the Bishop's. It also said what a terrible state they were in. Jude didn't know for sure whether or not VA10 had worked. It certainly didn't sound that way from what Father Williams had written. And let's not forget that as far as he knew, Sylvia had been declared insane. He and all the other Demons from Cruor Pharma must have believed that she had turned out just like all the other failed volunteers – that is until now." I looked over my shoulder towards Sylvia. She stood motionless in her cell. Turning back to Raven, I whispered, "I think Jude has been waiting back in the shadows – biding his time – waiting for Middleton to finally come up with a drug that would work. Ben told me that Doshia hadn't been seen for a long time. But I think he's been waiting right under their noses. Only they didn't realise Doshia can move from one body to the next. Take on anyone's persona – live in multiple bodies at any one time. So going back to keeping Jude locked up in that cell is pointless." I stared back out through the rain-splattered window. "We'll have to let him come with us. There is no other option at the moment. We can't fight against a Demon. But maybe Doctor Langstone can." I stepped off the bunk and sat down. My head was spinning and my eyelids lay heavy. I yawned. This was one jigsaw that seemed impossible to fix together. The only thing that made sense to me was to get Raven, Max, Sylvia, and myself to Doctor Langstone's – away from everyone else that was after us.

CHAPTER TWENTY SIX

I had only been sitting down for a minute when the door to the cellblock opened. I jumped up. That jittery feeling rushed through me. We all headed for our cell doors, clinging onto the bars liked caged animals waiting to get out. I looked at Max, who nervously watched Dave as he fumbled with his keys. My eyes fell upon the door which led into the cellblock. No sign of Eric. I looked at Jude. He had his head pressed against the bars so he could peer down the centre aisle between the rows of cells. Pretending that I didn't know his secret was going to be hard. For every time I went along with his lies, it felt like I was turning a blind eye to what he'd done to Hannah. But I had to snap out of these conflicting feelings – stop thinking about Hannah. I couldn't let them cloud my head – not when I needed a clear mind. My main focus for now was to get out of this police station and reach Doctor Langstone. Then, I would deal with Jude. I didn't know how, but some way I would make him pay.

As I stood quietly with thoughts of revenge and rage churning up inside my head, I was suddenly aware of Raven standing beside me. She gripped hold of the bars. I could feel her tense up as Dave finally found the correct key for Max's cell.

"I'm gonna put you over here in this cell," he said, pointing towards the one next to Jude. "Someone will be down soon to clean up this mess." His eyes wandered from Max over to Sylvia who had stayed perfectly quiet since attacking the drunk man. I shivered as my eyes locked on hers. She stared in silence and it was the quiet that frightened me. It was threatening – intimidating. For behind that silence, was something terrible. You could see it in her eyes. She was calculating – not just the crazy inmate from the asylum who didn't know what she was doing. No, she was working things out – checking us all out – planning her next move. I didn't want to take her with us but something in me said I needed to.

I was shaken out of my thoughts by Max, his voice echoed through the cellblock.

"What about her?" Max asked, staring at Sylvia. "Who's gonna clean her up?" His gaze drifted up to the blood around her mouth and down to the red clumps of flesh stuck to her hospital gown.

"No one here." Dave grimaced. "I should imagine the Sergeant will have her carted back to the asylum as soon as that Inspector has spoken to her."

"What Inspector?" Jude suddenly piped in.

"Inspector Cropper – the one who's interested in you lot," answered Dave.

I saw the worry in Jude's face at the mention of Cropper. We were all worried by the thought of Inspector Cropper, but of course, it would mean a lot more to Jude if he truly was Doshia. I smiled to myself at seeing his discomfort at the possibility of losing the lead in gaining us for the Cleaners. If Cropper got us, then we would be taken back to Cruor Pharma and Doctor Middleton would be the winner in all this. But would that make Jude more dangerous, knowing that he was running out of time? Would he do something more drastic?

"Must be mad himself if he thinks he's gonna get any answers from her," I heard Dave say. He stood and looked at us. "That Inspector reckons he's been trying to get her released for the last three months for questioning – just like the Sarge." He paused for a moment and slowly shook his head. "I don't know what you lot have been up to in Holly Tree, but Eric reckons that Inspector was desperate for us to keep you held here until he could get to Carden." He took a deep breath, key poised in front of the lock on Max's cell. "For what it's worth, I don't see how you lot could have caused so much carnage down in that train tunnel." He stopped talking and stared at us as if waiting for some kind of explanation. When nothing was offered up, he shrugged and pushed the key into the lock.

I almost felt bad knowing what Max was going to do and hearing Dave not believing that we had been responsible for all those deaths made me feel guilty – guilty for what was about to happen. For if he thought we were innocent now – he wouldn't soon.

The key turning in the lock sounded through the cellblock over-riding the constant fall of rain against the windows. I could hear Raven muttering under her breath – urging Dave to hurry up and open Max's cell. The tension was unbearable. We all seemed to take a step back – breaths held.

The cell door opened and Max stepped out. Could he overpower Dave? Max's frame, although toned, was not muscular, not like Dave's who was thick-set and a couple of inches taller. Not to mention that Dave had probably been trained in some kind of self-defence and ways to restrain criminals. He wore a belt with all sorts of equipment that could aid him in keeping hold of a prisoner.

I watched closely as Dave wandered down past the cells, until he stopped outside the one next to Jude. My eyes darted nervously back to the door leading into the cellblock. Would Eric suddenly walk in and make an appearance? Turning back, I caught Max's eyes. I gave him a reassuring nod as I could see the doubt in his stare. "You can do it," I mouthed silently at him.

Dave unlocked the cell. "In you go." He stepped aside.

Max hesitated. He knew too well that the moment he stepped into that cell would be the end of our escape, but how was he going to tackle Dave front on? Raven must have realised Max's predicament as she suddenly called out.

"Hey, Dave," she said, trying to get his attention away from Max. She suddenly leapt on me and started screaming. "I'm gonna fucking kill her!" Before I even had a chance to realise what was going on, Raven had toppled me down to the floor and was pulling at my hair. She screamed and yelled in my face, fistfuls of my hair screwed up tightly in her hands.

In the struggle, I caught sight of Dave, his attention no longer on Max but staring wide-eyed at Raven and me. His back was now turned towards Max. This was our chance – Max's only opportunity to attack Dave and get him locked away inside the cell.

Dave opened his mouth to say something, but before he could, Max had swiped a small canister from Dave's belt. As Dave swung around to confront him, Max pressed down on the top of the canister and sprayed some of the contents of the bottle. A fine mist shot directly into Dave's face. He waved his arms around as if trying to disperse the spray, but it was too late. He started yelling and coughing. His hands clawed at the skin around his eyes.

"Get him!" shouted Raven, letting go of me and jumping back to her feet. She clung onto the bars. "Push him into the cell – do it!"

Max lunged forward, grabbing hold of Dave by the shoulders and pulled him towards the cell door.

"Take his radio," ordered Jude. "And get those handcuffs on him."

"Knock him out!" snarled Raven. She jumped up and down on the spot, her knuckles white from the grip she had on the bars. She looked like a spectator at a boxing match.

I clambered back to my feet. I could hear Max gasping as he tried to use all of his weight to pull Dave into the cell. Dave staggered forwards but not enough. He tipped left and right just in the doorway, his hands rubbing franticly at his sore eyes. His breathing was laboured like he was having an asthma attack. I glanced back at the door leading into the cellblock, fearful that Eric would come running in from all the noise. The tension inside me leapt from my throat and I hollered, "Come on, Max, come on!" I jumped up and down alongside Raven, shaking the bars.

"I'm trying!" gasped Max, squeezing around Dave and coming at him from behind. He shoulder-barged Dave, knocking him further into the cell. I watched as Dave fell forward onto his knees. Max bent down and pulled the baton from off Dave's belt. He raised his arm, hesitated briefly, shut his eyes, and brought the baton down over the back of Dave's head. I cringed at the sound of impact. Dave fell to his side, toppling over and lying still in a heap.

"Take the radio!" shouted Jude again, waving his arms between the bars.

Max reached down and yanked the radio free. He passed it through the bars to Jude. Then bending down again, he removed the handcuffs and quickly secured them around Dave's wrists behind his back. He stood up, gasping. Satisfied that he had done what was needed to be done, he ran from the cell and closed the door, turning the key in its lock.

CHAPTER TWENTY SEVEN

"Open the door!" I yelled, my heart racing. I clung onto the bars and shook them. Raven pushed up behind me, desperate to get out.

"Come on!" she yelled, watching Max drop the keys as he fumbled around with them.

"I'm trying!" he said, looking flustered. He bent down and snatched them up. "Which key?" He held the metal ring up, which had a dozen or so different keys hanging from it.

"Just try any one," I said, feeling sick. My heart pumped fast and I could feel that sickly movement of VA20 shifting in me.

The first key didn't work. Neither did the second or the third. I heard Raven gasp in frustration as the fourth and fifth didn't turn either in the lock.

"Fucking hell!" hissed Raven. "Hurry up!"

I could see Max's hand shaking. He was a bundle of nerves. Reaching through the bars, I grabbed hold of his hand and said, "It's all right, you'll find the right one in a minute, nice and calm."

Max nodded his head and let out a deep sigh, like someone preparing to cut a wire attached to a bomb but not really knowing if it was the right one. He slipped the sixth key in and it turned. The sound of metal clicking in the lock was like heaven.

Raven and I pushed open the door and joined Max. He then went to where Jude was locked up. Unsure as to whether he should let him out, he looked at me, waiting for my response. I nodded my head. He pushed the first key in. Again it didn't work. After the fourth try, the lock came undone and Jude walked out.

We stood and looked at each other, not really knowing what to do. Then as if it suddenly all dawned on us that we didn't have time to just stand about, we kicked into action.

I reached down and snatched up the canister that Max had used on Dave. I pushed it into my pocket. Max tucked the baton down the inside of his jeans and Jude slipped the radio into his trouser pocket.

"Everyone remember the way out?" I asked, my stomach knotted up. How we were going to get through the Custody Suite without being seen, I had no idea.

"Yes," answered Raven.

The silence in the cellblock was suddenly broken. Dave's radio hissed into life. The voice on the other end sounded muffled. Jude pulled it out from his pocket.

"Dave... come in, Dave... where are you?"

"Eric," I whispered, afraid that I could be heard coming through the radio.

"Dave... you still in the cellblock?"

"Someone needs to answer," I pushed, looking at Max and Jude. "Or he's gonna come looking in here for Dave."

"We don't sound nothing like Dave," whispered Max, holding his hands out as if in need of help.

"Well, don't look at me," said Jude. "Neither do I."

"Dave... come in, mate... is everything all right?"

"Stop fucking about and one of you answer," I snapped, panic eating my insides up.

"Do it!" hissed Raven, towering over the lot of us.

Jude pushed the radio towards Max. Max pushed it back.

"Give it to me!" Raven snatched the radio and pressed the button on top. "I'm fine... thanks, Eric," she spoke deeply into the radio. She didn't sound like a man at all.

We stood huddled together, waiting for Eric to respond. The radio hissed.

"I'm on my way down to the cellblock." The radio cut off.

Holding her thumb over the button, she pressed it down and spoke again. "No need... I'm heading out now... going to... to... the dog unit."

"Dog unit?" questioned Jude, screwing his nose up. "Do they even have a dog unit here?"

"How the hell should I know?" hissed Raven. "It was the first thing that came into my head."

"He's not responding," I said, looking at the door. Any minute now and Eric would be walking into the cellblock.

A low moan came from the cell where Dave was locked in. I stepped away and leant up against the bars. "He's coming round... he's gonna yell this whole place down."

"Go back in there and knock him out again," snapped Raven, pushing Max towards the cell.

"No way – I'm not doing that again," argued Max, his eyes wide at the very thought. "I don't want to kill the guy."

"I'll do it then," hissed Raven, snatching the keys from Max.

"No!" I shouted. I curled my fingers around the metal ring and pulled the keys away from Raven. "We haven't got time, Raven. Eric is on his way and..." Before I could finish the sentence, I was pulled back violently. My head hit the bars. Two hands with bloody fingertips snaked their way around my neck and gripped me by the throat. I had been too preoccupied with our escape to realise that I had backed myself up against Sylvia's cell. I instinctively threw my hands up to my throat, my fingers trying to prise Sylvia's grip away from me.

I was suddenly crowded around by Jude, Max, and Raven as they tried to release me from Sylvia. Her hold was too strong. I tried to pull away, but each time I strained forward, Sylvia would yank me back, smashing my head hard against the bars.

"Snap her fingers back," I heard Max yell at Jude as he tried to prise his fingers in between my neck and Sylvia's hold.

"I'm trying!" struggled Jude. "Her fingers are too bloody... I can't get a good grip."

I gasped in a mouthful of air as the pressure against my throat loosened momentarily. I had to get her off. Bringing my arms up above my head, I bent them back and pushed them between the bars. My hands waved about, snatching at nothing but air until my fingers found the sides of Sylvia's head. I grabbed a handful of hair in each palm, clawing my fingers through the knots until I reached her scalp, then pulling forward with all my strength, I bashed her forehead into the bars, over and over. She still wouldn't let go.

"Mind your head!" Max suddenly shouted. Before I could even blink, Jude pulled my head to the left. The baton just missed me as it was shoved through, smacking into Sylvia's crazy face. Max pulled it back out and then again, holding it with both hands, like he was holding a snooker cue. He forced it at speed back into Sylvia. I stumbled forward as her bloody fingers fell away.

I leapt up and spun around. Sylvia staggered about in her cell, dazed and stunned.

"Let's get out of here," urged Max, tucking the baton back inside his jeans.

"Wait!" shouted Raven. "What about her?" She pointed at Sylvia. "We need her."

"We don't need that kind of shit!" argued Max. "Are you out of your mind?"

"We do need her," said Jude. "If we don't take Sylvia, then she'll either end up locked away in the asylum forever, or worse, she'll be another body for the Cleaners to take. That's not good for us."

I eyed Jude. I knew what he was up to. Of course he didn't want to leave her behind. But it wasn't for our benefit – just his. My mind felt scrambled. Ben had got her out – so she must be important. I could see that if we took her with us, it would stop Middleton from having her...but what about Jude? I paced up and down. My mind felt stretched in so many ways and not having time to think it through properly didn't help. I had to make a quick decision.

"We can't take her!" argued Max. "The moment you let her out, she's gonna go on a killing spree... us being her first victims!"

A sudden gust of wind rattled the cell windows, making the rain fall against the glass like someone had just thrown a bucket of water against them. Dave moaned again. We fell into silence, almost afraid of waking Dave fully.

"I say take her!" whispered Raven.

Max looked around at each of us, his body tense, eyes edgy. "I say you're out of your fucking minds!"

"Well?" Jude looked at me.

Before I could answer, the sound of footsteps clumping down the corridor just outside the cellblock had us all turning around. We watched as the door handle slowly turned.

CHAPTER TWENTY EIGHT

We scattered. Pushed up against the wall on either side of the door, me with Max one side, Jude and Raven on the other. I gripped the canister in my hand and watched Max slide out the baton. I prayed it was only Eric and he hadn't alerted any of the other officers. We could handle one easily.

I waited. The door opened a gap. Two voices broke through. I felt my heart flutter at the sound. We could handle two – couldn't we? I took a deep breath. It was definitely Eric I could hear. The other voice belonged to a female. It was probably Grace who I had seen in the custody suite when we had first been brought in.

The door opened fully.

"Dave?" Eric stepped in, Grace right behind him. We stood frozen to the spot. Any minute now, they would turn, catch a glimpse and see us. The door swung shut behind them.

"The cells have been opened!" exclaimed Grace, taking another step forward. "Where are the prisoners... where's Dave?"

Jude didn't wait to be spotted. He leapt out from his hiding spot and threw himself onto Eric. I heard Grace scream. She reached for her radio. I flung myself onto her back. Max swung the baton, knocking the radio from her hand. Wrapping my legs tight about her, she toppled left, then right. Raven came charging across the floor. She barged into Grace, throwing her off balance. She fell sideways into the bars of a cell, the both of us hitting the floor together. As Grace tried to get up, I snatched at her face, my nails slicing through her skin. As Raven and I struggled to keep Grace down, from the corner of my eye, I saw Eric take a blow to the side of his head as Max swung the baton down. Eric wobbled slightly but still remained standing. I continued to struggle with Grace. She wriggled out of my grip and kicked out her legs, taking Raven down in one swipe. As she threw herself across the floor, her arm outstretched for the radio, I clambered to my feet. I kicked the radio like I was scoring a goal. It flew up into the air, smashed into the wall, and broke apart. The pieces fell to the floor. I turned my attention back to Grace. She was pulling out her baton. Raven whipped around behind Grace and wrapped her arms about her. She held her tight around the neck in an arm lock.

"Do it!" screamed Raven, staring wide-eyed at me. Her eyes had that red mist clouding them again. Grace wriggled and tried to free herself from Raven's hold. "Hit her!"

"If you hit me…" gasped Grace, "then you'll be in even more trouble for assaulting a police officer!" Her eyes bulged as Raven tightened her grip.

"I'm already in the shit," I spat. "This is nothing compared to what I've already been framed for!"

I pulled my arm back and clenched my fist. I felt my knuckles hit bone as they pounded into Grace's head.

"Again!" Raven yelled, her face dark with anger. "Knock her out!"

I knew I wouldn't be able to do that with my punch alone, so I reached down and gripped hold of the baton lying beside Grace. I could feel VA20 rush through me – anger, fury, rage. The emotions hit me and I screamed out as I swung the baton straight into Grace's face. She immediately fell limp in Raven's arms. Blood poured from her nose and ran down into her open mouth. I watched as Raven tossed her aside. My head pounded and my limbs shook. But it wasn't over yet. My eyes fell on Eric. He stood with his back to me, egging on Max and Jude, his body language bolshie and arrogant, shoving his fists and knocking them into Max. I reached for the metal bars of a cell to steady myself. Whatever was going on inside me, it filled me with an annoyance, an irritation, and right now, that irritation was Eric. I hadn't forgotten the things he'd said to us earlier on. His words lay deep-rooted and I found myself standing behind him without even realising that I had moved.

"Eric!" I screamed behind him. He stopped fighting with Jude and Max. He spun around clearly shaken.

Being the arsehole that he was, he regained some composure and stared back, a defiance in those smug eyes of his. His top lip curled up in a sneer.

"Got something to say, you filthy crackhead?" He looked me up and down as though I was nothing but filth from the bottom of his shoe. "I ain't got no needles for you to stick in those ugly, repulsive veins." His eyes glimmered as if he had got one over me. Deep down, he had. Those words hurt more than any physical pain I had felt. He caught me off-guard as I rose my hand up to the side of my neck – a natural instinct that I had seemed to develop since the appearance of those black veins. I wanted to cover them up – pretend they weren't there. As my fingers slid up the side of my neck, I felt a sharp sting to the side of my face. The next thing I knew, I was half lying–half propped up against a cell. Eric had slapped me clean over and had now knocked Max from off his feet. I shook my head, feeling stunned. As I tried to clear my mind, something in the corner of my eye made my heart stop. Bare feet shuffled past me. My eyes rose to see Sylvia out of her cell. I gasped in shallow breaths. I wanted to get up – to run, but I couldn't seem to move. I felt petrified – frozen in time. I glanced back at her cell. How had she opened the door?

"Sylvia's out!" I yelled. No one heard me. They we're still fighting. Sylvia snapped her head round and stared at me. I felt myself shrink back. I glanced about the cellblock to see if there was something I could use – anything to stop her from hurting the others. I pulled out the canister from my pocket – no, that wouldn't do. I would have to get up close to Sylvia for it to have any effect and I didn't fancy coming face to face with her. The baton still lay beside Grace. I scrambled on my hands and knees, my body jittery. As I grasped hold of the baton, I heard someone scream. Moving quickly, I struggled onto my feet. Sylvia wrenched Eric away from Jude and Raven. I watched in horror as she scuttled up the wall dragging Eric with her. One hand had disappeared into his chest, while the other hand was used to manoeuvre herself up the side of the cellblock. He yelled out in pain as each movement ripped open his chest some more. Smears of blood were trailed up the wall. Flashbacks of Cruor Pharma and its dark corridors flickered on and off. Those bloody handprints I had come to dread were now back in front of me.

"Let's go!" I screamed, pulling Max to his feet.

"Help me!" gurgled Eric, his arms flapped loosely as Sylvia pinned him to the ceiling. A shower of blood sprayed from Eric like a fire sprinkler attached to the ceiling.

I looked away feeling sick. There was no helping Eric, and besides, I didn't want to. "Come on!" I yelled at Raven and Jude, who stood watching Sylvia.

"We have to wait for Sylvia." Jude was persistent.

"Fine," I snapped, "you wait for that freak – we're going." I snatched hold of Raven's arm. "Move or we leave without you." Time was running out and we still had to get through custody. I no longer cared of Sylvia's importance. Jude or Doshia could have her. And if Ben needed her so much then he could come and get her. Taking hold of Raven and Max, I marched them to the door. Pulling it open, I ran out into the corridor.

CHAPTER TWENTY NINE

"Let's get out of here before Sylvia comes after us," I whispered, aware that we shouldn't make too much noise. I knew the police station seemed to be short of officers and we'd just removed three of them out of the picture, but the Sergeant was probably still in the custody suite and all he had to do was get onto his radio and call for back-up.

We reached the end of the corridor. Max held his ear up to the door.

"Can you hear anything?" I whispered, looking over my shoulder, afraid I would see Sylvia scampering along the walls towards us.

"It's quiet," hushed Max. "I can't hear anyone." His eyes fixed on the door leading back into the cellblock. I knew he feared Sylvia like I did. His face was pale and sweaty and his hands shook.

"Let's go then," I said, taking hold of the door handle.

"Wait!" Max whispered. He pushed his ear back against the door. "I think there is someone in there."

Peering back towards the cellblock, I said, "I'd rather take my chances with whoever is in the custody suite. I'm not waiting for Sylvia to appear."

"Hold on," said Raven, grabbing hold of my hand. "Perhaps we should send Sylvia in there – she'd soon get rid of anyone who might get in our way."

"No – no way!" Max shook his head. "She'll kill us first before she starts in there."

"She's not a trained guard dog, Raven," I whispered. "She doesn't follow instructions. You think that if we tell her to leave us alone and only attack who we tell her to, she's going to comply – feed her a treat and she'll obey?" I turned the door handle.

"We keep out of her way," argued Raven. "Keep that door open and she'll go charging in – job done!"

"Keep out of her way? We're stuck in a narrow corridor, in case you haven't realised. The only place we can stand is in here – pushed up against the walls – we'll just breathe in and hope she doesn't notice us!" I snapped.

"We haven't got time for this," whispered Max, leaning in close. "Cropper will be here soon. We have to get out of this police station before he gets here. It won't just be him either that turns up – he's bound to bring the rest of his bent team with him."

"This is the perfect opportunity to get away from Sylvia and from Jude," I said. "If we don't go now... then..."

The door leading into the cellblock slowly creeped open. We turned towards it. Jude stood just inside the doorway, Sylvia behind him.

"Don't panic," said Jude. "She's handcuffed. She can't hurt you."

"How the hell did you get those cuffs on her?" gasped Max.

"Doesn't matter, does it?" said Jude. "What does matter is that we now have Sylvia and we're free of the cells."

"She can't hurt us?" I almost laughed. What the fuck was Jude on? She still had legs – teeth – arms that still had some free movement. Of course she could hurt us.

"She's quietened down a bit too, you know – trance-like." Jude took hold of the handcuffs and led Sylvia out into the corridor, like a stable hand leading a horse from a field. She staggered forwards, her blood-spotted eyes twitching up and down – left to right. "So, what's the plan?"

"We get our stuff... and we leave," said Raven, glaring at Jude. She glanced at me with a smile across her face. "Look what I've got!" She pulled a set of keys from out of her pocket and waved them about in the air. The narrow corridor echoed with the sound of the keys jangling.

"What are they for?" whispered Max, taking hold of them.

"Eric dropped his keys," smiled Raven. "I think the key to the van is on here."

"Great," grinned Jude. He reached out to take the keys from Max, but before he could, I snatched them away.

"I'll take them," I said, placing them inside my pocket.

"I can drive," pushed Jude, holding out his hand.

"So can I," I smiled. There was no way I was going to let him take the wheel. I had every intention of getting to Doctor Langstone and I didn't trust Jude any longer to get us there. "You can sit in the back of the van with her!" I glanced at Sylvia. She stood motionless. "Right, let's go." I turned the door handle and pushed it open just a gap. My eyes searched the custody suite. All seemed very still. I looked at the counter. The sound of paperwork being shuffled came from behind the desk. As I peered around the door, I could see the Sergeant filing away sheets of paper. He had his back turned towards me. Leaning away from the gap in the door, I whispered, "The

Sergeant's behind the desk. It's just him in there."

"Just go," pushed Raven, shoving me in the back.

"Stop it," I whispered, knocking her arm away. "We do this quietly. Ready?"

Everyone nodded except Sylvia. She had started to sway on the balls of her feet. I turned my attention back to the custody suite. Edging the door open slowly, I stepped out into the room. The light was brighter compared to the dark corridor we had just been standing in. I kept my eyes firmly on the Sergeant. The others filed out slowly – Sylvia shuffled out last.

We edged our way towards the desk. One step at a time, careful to stay quiet. Every movement from the Sergeant had us stopping, breaths held. Would he turn around? Was he going to see us before we could reach him? It was like a game of Peep-Behind-the-Curtain, trying to stay silent but having to move quickly.

I spotted our stuff behind the desk. It had been placed in clear plastic bags and put onto a shelf. As I took another step forward, the Sergeant suddenly turned around. His eyes stretched wide at the sight of us and he nearly stumbled over. In a fluster, he reached for his radio.

I sprung forward and hurled myself up onto

the desk. Max joined me. We swung our legs over the counter and threw ourselves onto the Sergeant. His fingers snatched for the radio but he couldn't quite reach it.

"No you don't!" I shouted, taking hold of his arm and pulling it away.

"Get off!" shouted the Sergeant, swiping his arms about and hitting me in the face. I staggered back but regained my footing. I lunged at him. Max pulled out the baton from his jeans.

As we struggled to restrain him, Jude leapt up and over the desk, snatching the Sergeant's head. He rammed it down onto the counter.

"Dave... Grace...!" the Sergeant called out. Blood gushed from his nose.

Reaching into my pocket, I yanked out the canister and as Jude pulled up the Sergeant's head, I pressed the button and sprayed.

The custody suite was filled with the sound of the Sergeant's coughing and choking. He immediately stopped fighting and slowly slid from the desk onto the floor. He lay, clawing at his throat, his breathing nothing more than short, sharp gasps.

I bent over him and took his handcuffs, snapping them onto his wrists. I stood up and grabbed the plastic bags from off the shelf.

Throwing them over the desk, I took one last look at the Sergeant. Max smashed the baton down. I heard the sound of bone splitting and my stomach lurched. The sergeant stopped struggling and fell still.

"Okay," I breathed, "let's go." I climbed back over the desk and dropped to the floor. "Come on – hurry up." I felt nervous, that panicky feeling chomped away at my insides. I looked at Raven. She had already removed Hannah's leather jacket from out of one of the plastic bags and had put it on. She zipped up the front, covering up the flowery blouse that she hated so much.

Sylvia had shuffled over to the door which led out to the yard. She swayed on her feet, mumbling something under her breath. Did she even know what was happening?

"Get the keys ready!" shouted Max, snatching up the clear plastic bags.

I pulled them out from my pocket. There were a lot of keys that looked like the sort you would use for a van, but which one was right, I had no idea.

"What about our shoes?" Max blurted out, holding up one of the clear plastic bags.

"No time for shoes!" shouted Jude. "Let's just find the van and go."

"We'll put them on when we get out of here," I said, running over to the door.

Raven turned the door handle and yanked it open. The corridor leading out into the yard was empty. I breathed a sigh of relief. We were almost there. Almost out of the police station.

We ran down the corridor. As I reached the door to our freedom, I looked over my shoulder just to make sure we were all still together. Satisfied that we hadn't left anyone or any of our things behind, I stepped out into the cold, wet night.

CHAPTER THIRTY

The rain hit me like hundreds of tiny needles peppering my skin. I shielded my eyes from the gusts of wind as it threw up my hair into a tangled mess. My bare feet sloshed through the cold puddles that swelled in large pools across the yard.

Where was the van? I spun around feeling lost. The dark, the rain and the wind disorientated me.

"Over here!" Raven called out. She had darted around the side of the police station and now I could just see her head poking around the corner of the building. Her hair lashed about her head like slick, angry tentacles.

I hunched forward, trying to block out the wind as it whipped about me. I jumped over the puddles, Max at my side. The slosh of water behind me let me know that Jude and Sylvia were close behind. As I reached Raven, another sharp gust of wind nearly blew me off my feet. I turned down the side of the building. My eyes looked in dismay at the row of police vans parked in the bays. Which one was ours? Which key was the right one?

"Hurry up!" cried Raven over the sound of

the thrashing wind.

I pulled out the keys from my pocket. Feeling panicked and knowing that we probably didn't have much time left before Cropper arrived, I leapt into action. The first van wasn't ours. After trying each key in the lock and failing to open it, I moved on to the next one. My hands were frozen and I dropped the keys several times. The others gathered around me. I could see in their wind-battered faces, the sheer will for me to find the right van. Only Sylvia hung back. She stood in the middle of a puddle, her white hospital gown flaying about. The handcuffs around her wrists glinting every so often from the floodlights that twitched on randomly. She watched in silence, not even flinching from the unrelenting wind.

"Next van!" hollered Jude, after I had tried every key.

I sloshed through the puddles, my feet feeling numb from the cold. This was the third van. I prayed it was the one.

"Third time lucky?" Max said, hope in his eyes. His T-shirt clung to him like he had just climbed out of a swimming pool. He shivered – his limbs jerked uncontrollably.

"Come on!" shrieked Raven, her annoyance directed at me as I dropped the keys again.

"I'm trying!" I glared. "My hands hurt… I'm so cold."

I pushed the key into the lock. It wouldn't turn. Pulling it out, I tried another and then another. Shaking my head and using my arm to rub away the stream of rain water flowing down my face, I looked at the others. It seemed hopeless.

"There's still two more vans!" shouted Jude, stumbling forward as the wind buffeted into him. He disappeared around the side of the van.

Raven stomped her foot down, sending up a spray of rain. "This has to be it – it must be!"

As the wind battered its way across the yard, another noise joined in the gusts.

I blinked, the rain stung my eyes. "What was that?"

We stood still, straining to hear over the blasts of the punishing storm. It sounded like a metal grating noise. The yard was suddenly filled with two cones of light.

"It's a vehicle… maybe a police car… it could be the night shift?" shouted Max, trying to hold back his hair that twisted and coiled about his face.

"It could be Cropper!" yelled Jude, running over to where Sylvia still stood. He grabbed hold of the handcuffs and pulled her over to where we stood. "Keep trying the vans! We'll keep watch."

My fingers nervously twitched over the keys. I shook my hair from out of my face. First one didn't work, second – nope – third. "Fucking hell!" I yelled out in frustration. My foot kicked out at the van. None of the keys worked. I would have to go around to the last van. "Can you see anyone?" I called out.

Raven, Jude, and Max were crouched down, peering around the side of the van. I flinched as the two cones of light swerved around the side of the building. "Shit!" I pushed myself up against the van, trying to make myself invisible. Forgetting my fear of Sylvia, I grabbed hold of her and pulled her alongside me. Her bedraggled hair clung to the sides of her face. She leered out at me with her blood-spotted eyes. "Don't move," I warned her. Whether she understood me, I had no idea, but if I didn't keep her out of sight then we would all get caught.

Max crawled away from the spot where he had been crouching. He reached me and looked up, wobbling on his feet as the wind rushed down between the vans.

"It's Cropper," he said, a grave look across his face. "He has another police officer with him."

"Are they still in the car?" I asked, my teeth chattering.

"They've just got out," said Max, cupping his hands around his mouth like a funnel so I could hear him over the wind and rain.

"Have you tried this van?" asked Max.

"Yes... it's not the one," I answered. I looked about me. I couldn't go around the front of this van to reach the last one for fear of being spotted by Cropper. I would have to clamber my way around the back of it.

"Keep trying, Kassidy," shuddered Max. "It won't be long before Cropper realises we've escaped. He'll be back out here looking for us."

I nodded my head and shifted along the van, keeping my back pressed tight about it. There was a small gap between the wall and the back of the van and I squeezed through. Checking that I couldn't be seen, I slid along to the door of the last van. I jumped. Sylvia had followed me. She stood against the wall, her hair sprayed up like waves hitting a cliff. Her expression was dead, yet her eyes had something in them. She knew more than she let on. I was sure of it. A blast of wind woke me from my thoughts and I looked away from her. I didn't have time to keep my eyes on what she was up to. I fumbled with the keys. This had to be the van and I rushed as fast as I could with each key. "Come on... come on," I mumbled, pushing the last key into the lock. "No!" I yelled out, not believing that it wouldn't turn. I pulled it out and shoved it back in again. It had to work... it was the last van. I glanced over my shoulder. There was no sign of Cropper, yet. But a few more minutes and all hell would break out. I stared at the keys. Had there been one that I'd missed? I glanced to my left and nearly dropped the keys again. Sylvia was standing beside me. Her mouth was turned up into a grin. Not a happy one but an evil one. She started to laugh. I stepped away. Sylvia slowly lifted up her arms. The handcuffs rattled as she pointed a finger across the yard. Almost too afraid to look away, I slowly turned my head. I squinted against the onslaught of rain as it pelted my face in angry waves. What was she pointing at? The yard was so dark and what with the stormy weather, it was hard to see. "What? What is it?"

The handcuffs rattled again and I could hear Sylvia slowly chuckle.

"I don't have time for this..." I snapped, my eyes suddenly catching sight of something white, hidden beneath a low set of hanging branches, towards the back of the yard. I felt my heart leap. It was another van. I swung round and stared at Sylvia in surprise. Was she trying to help me? Or was she just laughing at my incompetence? Had she known all along that there was another van? There wasn't time to figure it out. I called to the others, "Max, Raven… Jude!"

"Is this it?" asked Raven, looking like a drowned rat as they appeared from the back of the van. She stared at the vehicle beside me.

I shook my head, "No… it must be that one." I pointed across the yard. "Come on, we have to try."

"Wait," called Jude. "Make sure it's all clear first." He peered around the front of the van. "Clear… let's go!" He darted across the yard sending up sprays of rain water. Raven followed and disappeared into the dark.

I looked at Max and then my eyes met Sylvia's. It suddenly dawned on me that I would have to get her across the yard, but how? She didn't move too fast.

"Max, you're gonna have to help me," I called, stumbling to my right as the wind forced its way down between the two vans. "You take one side and I'll take the other." I gripped hold of Sylvia's arm. Max looked unsure but he did it.

"You ready?" I asked stepping out of our hiding place and into the open of the yard.

Max nodded his head. We didn't run. It was more like a trot. Sylvia dragged her feet through the puddles. Every so often, she would snigger to herself. I glanced over my shoulder every few seconds, expecting to see Cropper appear. I let out a sigh of relief as we reached the other side of the yard. The branches swayed about, smacking into the roof of the van, sending a shower of wet leaves tumbling down. I took hold of the first key and pushed it into the lock. It didn't turn. I tried the next one, lowering my head as a large branch swooped down. The van wobbled as another large gust of wind slapped into the side of it.

"Keep watch," I ordered, fumbling with the keys. If only my hands weren't so cold. My fingers had stiffened up like a corpse's.

The third key slid into the lock and I heard a gasp of relief from my friends as it turned, releasing the locks.

I yanked open the driver's door and climbed in, slamming it behind me. A cold chill hit me as the passenger door flew open. Max and Raven climbed in. My hand trembled as I turned the ignition. The engine stuttered and died.

"Hurry up!" cried Raven.

"Shut up, I'm concentrating!" I yelled, turning the key again. The hatch behind me slid open and Jude poked his head through.

"Are you sure you can drive?" His eyes met

mine. I glared at him.

"Fuck off," I snapped, pressing my foot down on the accelerator as the engine rumbled into life. "You just worry about keeping Sylvia calm." I pushed the gear into first and slowly released the clutch. It had been a while since I had been behind the wheel of a car, and never had I driven a van, especially with bare feet. The vehicle pulled away slowly, rocking slightly from the strength of the wind. As I turned it round, the shadowy figure of Cropper came running out of the door to the police station, followed by another officer.

"Cropper's seen us!" shouted Max. He leant across Raven and pushed down on the lock.

"How the hell do we get out of here?" I yelled, staring at the heavy iron gates. They were shut, blocking off our escape. I looked into my side mirror. Cropper was running across the yard. His bulbous eyes almost seemed to glow as the floodlights switched back on. My heart thumped heavy. I yanked on the gearstick, pulling it into reverse. My foot pressed down hard on the accelerator. I knew I didn't have any other choice but to try to break through the gates.

CHAPTER THIRTY ONE

As Inspector Cropper reached the back of the van, his fists hitting the back door, my foot was almost touching the floor. The wheels screamed over the roar of the engine. The windscreen was covered in sheets of rain and I flicked on the wipers.

"Put your seatbelts on!" I yelled. The van shot forward. "Hold on!"

"Shit!" screamed Max, bringing up his legs into the foetal position.

The iron gates came rushing at us. I gripped the steering wheel tightly and tensed in my seat waiting for impact. With one eye shut and my heart stuck in my throat, the bonnet smashed into the gates. The sound was deafening. The gates almost seemed to crumple outwards, as they were wrenched from their hinges. The van shot through and out onto the empty street. I smiled as I watched Cropper in the mirror get left behind. I turned to the right, the wheels screeching. The smell of burning rubber filled the van.

"I don't know which way to go," I snapped, fearful that I could mess up our escape if I took a wrong turn.

"Just keep on this main road," shouted Jude, his head still poking through the hatch.

I looked at Max. His hands gripped the dashboard tightly, his face white.

"We did it... we fucking did it!" squealed Raven, bouncing up and down in her seat. Her wet hair slapped around the sides of her face. It was the first time I had ever seen her look so happy.

"Don't get too excited," I said, keeping my eyes on the road. I looked down and checked my speed. I was doing 50 in a 30 zone. The shops of Carden whizzed by in a blur. "I won't feel excited until we find Doctor Langstone's. I don't even know what the hospital is called. Does it share the same name as Cruor Pharma?"

"I have no idea," answered Max, leaning back in his seat. He rubbed his arms with his hands.

"Put the heater on," I suggested. "We could all do with warming up." I noticed the goose bumps over my arms. The skin looked wrinkled from all the rain.

"I think I remember Nurse Jones mentioning the sister company," said Jude. "She called it Cruor Pharma."

I shifted in my seat. Of course, Jude would know what it was called. He had probably been there before. My mind started racing with thoughts about how we were going to ditch him – get rid of Doshia. But was there even a way?

A car horn suddenly blasted. I had shot through red lights and nearly hit a car turning across the road ahead of me.

"Shit!" I muttered. I didn't want to be involved in a crash – not now. Not when we were so close. I checked in my mirrors. We didn't seem to have anyone following us. I had half expected this escape to turn into one of those car chase programmes.

I was relieved to see that we were leaving the town of Carden. The shops had thinned out and as I stared through the wet windscreen, I could see dark, mountainous shadows on the horizon. I eased up on the accelerator. The roads had become narrow with tight bends to the left and right. Were we even heading in the right direction?

"Is Sylvia all right?" I asked, suddenly remembering that she was in the back with Jude.

"She's just sitting... zoned-out," answered Jude.

Raven leant forward and turned the radio on. She twiddled with the tuner until she found a song that she was happy with. The van filled with, *Faith in Love* by CSS. We sat quietly, lost in the song. My eyes stayed fixed to the road, fearful that

I may miss a road sign. The wipers worked fiercely to clear the rain, and as I started to relax a little, I saw something that had me sit bolt upright. Across the empty fields, I could just make out the first signs of fog.

"We'll have company soon," I said, my heart beginning to race again. Would the Cleaners ever give up?

"Who?" asked Jude.

"The Cleaners... look over to the left... across the field," I muttered, suddenly slamming my foot on the brake. The van skidded to a stop.

"What the hell are you doing?" hissed Raven. "I nearly smashed my face into the dashboard."

"Wouldn't make much difference," said Jude.

"Piss off!" Raven fumed.

"That road sign," I said, pointing across the narrow road and trying to see through the rain. "It says: *Cruor Pharma one mile*."

"That's it then," said Max. "We've found it... we've finally got here." He leant back in his seat and ran his fingers through his hair. I could see the anticipation in his eyes – the hope.

I started the van again, slowly taking the bends. My stomach was knotted up – head confused with conflicting feelings. I was relieved that we had got this far but scared at what we would find. Would Max finally be able to see his brother? Would he be alive and if so, was he like Sylvia? Would we be able to get rid of Doshia? Shouldn't we do it before we get into Cruor Pharma? And what about Ben? Was he still alive and would I see him again? But more importantly, would Doctor Langstone help us or would he take us, now that we were altogether? As I turned the van on a right bend, a small lane led off from the road. Another sign with *Cruor Pharma* printed across it pointed down the lane. I turned in. My head was full of questions – too many. Would I finally get some answers?

The van lurched over the bumps in the lane. We seemed to be heading downhill. Trees on either side of us swept across the windscreen. It was pitch-black, only the lights from the van seemed to exist out here. I peered through the window, half expecting something to come running out from the cover of the trees.

"I don't like it down here," whispered Raven. "It's like we're driving into the very pit of hell."

I didn't comment. No one did. But I think we all felt the same. As if out of nowhere, two large iron gates appeared. I slammed on the brakes.

"What does that say?" asked Max, squinting his eyes and staring ahead.

I leant forward in my seat. The iron lettering which formed part of the gates read, *Cruor Pharma*. There was a large iron chain which weaved through the bars. It was fixed together with a huge padlock.

"No one's home," Jude whispered.

"What do we do now?" I asked. I stared through the gaps in the bars, trying to see past it. It was too dark.

"We wait," answered Jude. "As soon as it gets light, we'll be able to see if anyone's about."

I looked at the others. I felt deflated. We had come so far and now we were here, we couldn't get in. As I peered out at the tall iron gates, the van lights illuminated the padlock. It looked ancient and rusty, like it hadn't been touched by human hands for a hundred years or more.

"This wasn't what I expected," I whispered, slumping back into my seat.

"What was you expecting?" asked Jude, his eyes peered at me from the mirror inside the van.

"For someone to be fucking home!" snapped Raven. "That would be a start."

"I don't know. I suppose I thought it would be more like the Cruor Pharma on Strangers Hill. You know – a night shift, a day shift, and cameras. At least more modern. But this!" I pointed at the gates. "This place looks deserted."

"It looks fucking dead!" sneered Raven.

"Could there be another entrance?" suggested Max, his eyes downcast.

"Don't think so," said Jude. "This is where the sign pointed us to. Why would there be another entrance?"

"We'll have to wait here until the morning," said Raven, her arms folded across her chest.

"We don't have time to wait." I leant forward so I could see Raven. "The fog will reach us by then."

Max shuddered as he peered out through the windscreen. "And do we really want to wait in the middle of nowhere... in the dark... Sylvia in the back?"

Jude looked over his shoulder into the back of the van. "She's handcuffed, she can't hurt us."

I wasn't so sure, and besides, I had no intention of trusting Jude's assurances. Shouldn't we be more concerned about being in the middle of nowhere with him? I tapped my fingers over the steering wheel.

Slapping his hand down onto my leg and making me jump, Max, eyes wide, gasped, "Look! What's that?"

My stare fell upon a flickering light someway off in the distance, behind the gates. I sat up straight. My stomach started to knot.

"What is it?" whispered Max.

As I peered through the windscreen, a dark shadowy shape seemed to float towards the gate. All my senses were telling me to leave – slam the van into first gear and pull away. But this is what we had come for – wasn't it? We needed help. Whatever was behind those gates was our only hope.

"Perhaps this place isn't as deserted as we first thought," I said under my breath. "It looks like someone or *something* is at home."

Damned (The Kassidy Bell Series) Book 4

Coming soon!

To connect with Lynda O'Rourke visit her facebook page at:
LyndaO'Rourkefacebook

Printed in Great Britain
by Amazon